They faced                  ned cottage, as                the roof.

"How quiet i      for the rain," said Damon. "I can almost hear what you're thinking. 'What will I do if he tries to kiss me? If he makes improper advances?' "

Beryl choked. "I was thinking no such thing!"

"Then you are very foolish and just as ignorant," Damon told her. "This is precisely the sort of situation that often figures in the dreams of a debauched gentleman like myself. No one is near to save you or to stop me."

He pulled her close, and Beryl melted into his arms, twining herself about his hard-muscled form. She didn't shrink when he pressed her to the floor. It was he who stopped himself, though his voice was still husky with passion when he said, "This is madness."

"If so, it is a delicious sort of madness," said Beryl, wondering who was seducing whom . . . and if either of them would be able to resist . . . ?

# Sweet Lavender

*by*

Margaret Evans Porter

A SIGNET BOOK

**SIGNET**
Published by the Penguin Group
Penguin Books USA Inc., 375 Hudson Street,
New York, New York 10014, U.S.A.
Penguin Books Ltd, 27 Wrights Lane,
London W8 5TZ, England
Penguin Books Australia Ltd, Ringwood,
Victoria, Australia
Penguin Books Canada Ltd, 10 Alcorn Avenue,
Toronto, Ontario, Canada M4V 3B2
Penguin Books (N.Z.) Ltd, 182–190 Wairau Road,
Auckland 10, New Zealand

Penguin Books Ltd, Registered Offices:
Harmondsworth, Middlesex, England

Published by Signet, an imprint of New American Library,
a division of Penguin Books USA Inc. Published by arrangement with
Walker & Company.

First Signet Printing, August, 1993
10 9 8 7 6 5 4 3 2 1

 REGISTERED TRADEMARK—MARCA REGISTRADA

Printed in the United States of America

# 1

*Damon was the pride of nature,*
*Charming in his every feature.*
                    —JOHN DRYDEN

All the world was headed for London, or so it seemed to Damon Lovell, Marquis of Elston, as his curricle wound its way deeper and deeper into the downland of West Sussex. Driving along the turnpike, he met a number of gigs, post chaises, and traveling carriages, all moving in the opposite direction, toward town.

His drab driving coat with fifteen capes at the collar, blue-and-yellow-striped waistcoat, and black-spotted cravat all designated him a member of the prestigious Four-in-Hand Club, but this was also apparent from his skilled handling of his horses. He had golden hair and eyes as blue as harebells, prominent cheekbones and a thin, aristocratic nose, the legacies of his great-grandmother, a Swedish countess and a famous court beauty during the reign of George the First.

Gently rolling hills gave way to picturesque, grass-covered escarpments, and by the time the curricle sped past Black Down, Damon had more or less resigned himself to the necessity of leaving town, where his friends were making merry. His sense of ill-usage, which had been strong at the outset of his journey, faded altogether when he inhaled the salt air. He was nearing the region where he'd passed part of his youth, and its landmarks were familiar to him.

Deerhurst, the home of the Kinnard family, was his destination on this glorious May afternoon. His errand was as much a mystery as it was an inconvenience, but when the Earl of Rowan's middle daughter, who was the wife of Damon's cousin, begged him to come to Sussex, he had not failed to comply. And he was sufficiently acquainted with Lady Louisa to know her trouble could be better explained in person.

"Dearest Damon," she had written, "I have removed from Fairdown and will reside at Deerhurst through the summer months. Roger has agreed to it. Ceddie has learned all they can teach him at Oxford and is now at home, and best of all, Sid and Tracy are expected on leave from these distressing wars. Do come! I *need* you desperately, ever so much more than you can imagine!"

Louisa's last sentence had clinched the matter, for to be needed was quite outside the realm of Damon's experience. Ordering his valet to pack at once, he had gone to the house of his mistress to break off a connection that had grown irksome of late, and departed London at an hour when he would normally have gone no farther than his own breakfast room.

After proceeding along a drive lined with towering beeches, he came to the house of aged brick. Square in design, it had been built in the simple, graceful Dutch style made fashionable by William and Mary, and looked southward. The front lawn was bare of ornamentation; on one side the grass gave way to woodland, and on the other was the stable block. As the curricle swept around a curve, Damon caught a glimpse of the parterres and formal landscaping behind the house, which had made Deerhurst a byword in a nation of gardeners.

Jessom, the earl's solemn butler, took Damon's hat, whip, and coat, and informed him that Lady Louisa was in the drawing room.

Her ladyship, a handsome brunette, lifted her beaming face for the kiss he claimed. "Dear Damon," she sighed thankfully, "I knew I might depend on you! You must have left London the instant you received my note!"

"I did," he replied, a fond smile softening his face.

"How well you look!"

"Permit me to return the compliment. Cousin Roger keeps his wife in a high state of preservation."

"Foolish boy," Louisa laughed, although in fact he was only a year younger than she. "If you but knew! He's busy morning, noon, and night with his crops and his cows, so I must amuse myself as best I can. Jack is all of six now, and very independent, and my Harry, who has turned three, is still very much under Nurse's thumb. Do you wonder that I deserted them all for the beauties of Deerhurst in the summer?"

"Yes, I do wonder," Damon told her frankly, taking a seat. "And I should also like to know why *my* presence should be so indispensable to you all of a sudden."

The lady settled herself more comfortably in her chair. "It's quite simple: our Beryl has become engaged. You can't imagine the trouble it makes."

"Surely Lady Beryl is of marriageable age by now."

"Lord, yes! In fact, she's perilously close to being on the shelf, for she's all of twenty-two. And she never had a season in town nor was she presented at court or—or anything!" Louisa glowered at the marquis, her bosom heaving with these injustices. "When she was eighteen, Papa said he preferred to wait another year before taking her to London. The following winter our mother died, and by the time we were out of mourning, both of my little ones came down with scarlet fever and I was tied to Fairdown. Then we lost John at Barrosa, and Beryl was in no state for balls and routs, nor was I. Still, I was determined she should see something of society, so this winter I prevailed upon Papa to let her go to York and Harrogate with Great-aunt Sophia. Which is why he holds me responsible for her coming home betrothed."

"Who is the fortunate fellow?" Damon asked.

"Mr. Peter Yeates—you don't know him; none of us knows him. He called on Papa in town, and very properly asked for Beryl's hand, not that it did him any good," she added on a bitter note. "Papa refused his consent. Unless he likes someone, he refuses to acknowledge their existence; so if we so much as mention the poor young man's name, his face turns the most alarming shade of red. His rages are likely to bring the roof down."

Damon, well acquainted with the turbulent earl, couldn't help smiling at this accurate if unfilial portrait. "What is his objection to your sister's choice?" he asked.

"Mr. Yeates's grandfather owns a manufactory. *And* made his fortune in trade," she said significantly.

"I see." And he did, for Lord Rowan was notoriously prejudiced against the rising middle class, which he was wont to deride as vulgar and money-grubbing.

"Papa says Beryl has more in common with a red-skinned savage than a man of Mr. Yeates's background, although from what she tells me he sounds perfectly respectable."

"Perhaps Lord Rowan will relent when he grows used to the idea," said Damon soothingly.

Louisa shook her head. "It isn't only Mr. Yeates he dislikes. Papa doesn't want Beryl to marry at all." She climbed to her feet and began pacing the room, her silken skirts whispering.

"But it is the duty of daughters to marry well. And, failing that, simply to marry."

"It isn't what Papa wants for his youngest daughter," she said firmly. "Damon, he dotes on her."

"Then I should think he would put her happiness above all other considerations."

"Unfortunately, it is otherwise. He will never, ever consider anyone good enough for Beryl. Well, to be fair, none of us would," she admitted with a slight shrug. "But Papa says so because he wants her to remain with him."

"Lady Beryl must be a remarkable young woman," Damon commented dryly.

"She is the dearest creature in all the world! So unfailingly good and patient, despite her illnesses—and they have been many."

That much he knew, for Louisa had never once written to him without some mention of the youngest Kinnard's precarious state of health, and dull reading it had been.

"Papa loves her the best of anyone on earth,"

she went on. "It isn't only that she's the baby of our family, and so pretty. She's just very ... lovable!"

Too polite to voice his true feelings on the subject, Damon said nothing, for he had judged Lady Beryl Kinnard as a most tiresome young woman. Why so sickly a creature should receive so much attention he could not imagine, although it was possible that the lively, healthy Kinnards had placed their runt and only weakling on a pedestal simply because her very difference was interesting to them.

The Earl of Rowan had nine children. Of the six sons, the eldest was married to a Cornish heiress, one was a parson in Northumberland, and three had gone into the Army; Damon remembered Cedric as a scruffy brat tagging at the heels of his brothers. The two eldest daughters were married, and the youngest of all the brood, memorable only for her unusual name, had been in the schoolroom at the time of Damon's last visit to Deerhurst.

Louisa continued mournfully, "So you see, my poor sister is engaged, and yet she isn't. She's not allowed to see Mr. Yeates, and he hasn't even written to her, not once. And, Damon, the very worst of it is that she bears it with the patience of a *saint*!"

"My dear Louisa," he said calmly, "if the situation disturbs you so, why don't you return to Fairdown?"

"Because Beryl needs me. Papa is determined to keep her buried here in Sussex, so I hit upon the notion of a summer house-party, thinking it might amuse her. You must help me make up my guest list, for my father refused his assistance—not that it matters. His friends are naught but old court cards like old Sir Harry Fetherstonhaugh at Up-park, and Lord Egremont, who talks of naught but painters and art the day long. You know so many interesting people, and I daresay a few of them would agree to come to Deerhurst."

She looked at him so expectantly he dared not point out that with the Season underway, her hope of assembling an interesting and fashionable party was little more than an air dream. "In your letter you said Sidney and Tracy were coming home on furlough. Aren't they capable of cheering your sister?"

"Brothers!" she said dismissively. "I have no patience with the breed. Did I tell you that Ceddie, foolish creature, has taken it into his head to write a novel? Don't laugh, it isn't a bit funny!"

"Ceddie? You can't be serious!"

"It's a fact. And a great nuisance, too, but you'll see for yourself."

Intrigued, he would have questioned her further, but at that moment another lady stepped into the room. Pausing on the threshold, she glanced at Damon and exclaimed, "Lord Elston, we didn't expect you so soon!"

Louisa went to put an arm about her sister's waist, bringing her forward. "Here, Damon, is our Beryl."

Damon had risen to his feet. The pretty intruder was not quite of medium height, with a neat figure and tiny waist, and her brown hair, worn longer than the fashion prevailing in town, was pulled back from a heart-shaped face. She had a small, upturned nose, tip-tilted green eyes set beneath arched brows, and a pair of peony lips.

Lady Beryl's voice was soft but carried no hint of shyness when she said, "So many years have passed since your last visit, my lord—I think you hardly remember me."

Before Damon could offer a civil and mendacious reply, Louisa asked eagerly, "Was there a letter in today's post?" Beryl nodded absently and continued to smile up at the visitor. "Oh, I'm so glad! All your doubts and fears can be laid to rest."

With a laugh, the young lady shook her head, and her long curls danced on her shoulders. "I feared nothing, Louisa, for I knew Mr. Yeates would write eventually. I'll tell you everything later, for I don't wish to bore Lord Elston with my affairs."

"'Lord Elston' indeed—he's Roger's cousin, child!"

"But not mine."

This reply startled Damon, and he supposed she was being deliberately pert. Her manners did not live up to her face, it seemed, so he decided to give her a demonstration of the proper mode. Sketching a bow, and without giving the least hint of his antipathy, he said smoothly, "Lady Beryl, your sister clearly feels that we must dispense with formality. I'd be honored if you would address me as 'cousin.'"

He was interrupted when a young man charged into the drawing room, crying, "Louisa, there's a chaise at the door, with a trunk strapped behind, and—oh, hullo, Damon!"

Louisa nodded. "That will be your man and your portmanteaux, Damon—pray excuse me. Ceddie, you've a smudge on your nose," she added before making her exit.

Her brother paid no attention, but stalked toward Beryl purposefully. "I understand Smith has brought the post-bag from the village. So, Beryl, have you received a letter from Mr. Yeates?"

"I have."

"Famous! If my heroine receives a *billet doux* at the outset of my story, it will make her separation from her lover all the more affecting."

"Well, it's not precisely a *billet doux*. You may read it if you must. But I left it upstairs."

Cedric shook his head at her. "You're supposed to keep the letter in the bosom of your gown, close to your heart. Have you *no* romantic sensibility?"

"Not much," Beryl said, reaching up to smooth his mussed hair, the same rich brown as her own. "If I did have, I shouldn't put up with your fashioning me as the heroine of your romance, so think on that, my good fellow!"

When she left the room, Damon said to the young man, "Louisa tells me you're a writer now."

"Oh, I am," Cedric replied enthusiastically. He held his pen carelessly by its point, unaware that the ink was rapidly staining his thin fingers. "At first I wanted to write a play, but it didn't prosper, so I made up my mind it should be a novel. I hope it will be as well received as the one Mr. Austen's sister wrote. She's already working on another." He met Damon's blank gaze and asked, "Have you not read *Sense and Sensibility*?"

With a deprecating shrug, Damon replied, "Novels are women's fare."

"You would like this one, I'm sure. But Miss Jane's authorship is supposed to be a secret. We only know of it because Papa banks with her brother's firm in London."

Lady Beryl soon returned with her letter, but she wouldn't give it to Cedric until he had used his handkerchief to wipe the ink from his hands.

"I may not keep it in the bosom of my gown," she said, her eyes bright, "but it *is* Mr. Yeates's first and only letter to me."

Her brother carried it out of the room, and Beryl laughed softly. "You can have no notion how very trying it is to be the heroine of a novel!" she told Damon. "My every move, my every thought is observed by Ceddie, and I can't sigh or smile without his asking me what I mean by it!"

His resentment of her was strong enough to withstand her sunny smile. "Doubtless he would prefer that you fall into a decline."

"Oh, I'd never dare to do that," she answered, "or my family would make my life a misery. As it is, I cannot take a tumble from my horse or give a sneeze that they don't wrap me in cotton wool!"

"Louisa has informed me that you do not enjoy the best of health, Lady Beryl." It was difficult to believe, however: her cheeks were delightfully pink and her green eyes so bright.

Her smile vanished. She regarded him silently for several seconds before saying, "My lord, I assure you that my delicacy exists only in my sister's over-anxious mind. And Papa's," she added quietly. "He stifles me with *his* kindness."

The unwilling recipient of this cryptic confidence was relieved when Louisa swept back into the room. After telling her sister it was high time to begin dressing, she turned to her guest. "You'd best heed my warning as well, Damon, for our father's temper only grows worse the longer he's kept from his dinner!"

The presence of company did not inspire Lady Beryl to attempt a fashionable toilette, and she came down to dinner simply attired in a blue muslin gown. Louisa, acting as her father's hostess, sat down at the head of the long table, and her siblings ranged themselves midway down, across from Damon. The earl, his nominal host, was the last to arrive, and while the butler and a full complement of footmen moved silently about the room, filling wine glasses and passing dishes, he greeted Damon by saying, "You'll be glad to get away from London, eh?"

Rather than refuting this false assumption, Damon answered, "The hectic activity of the season can be wearisome."

"I'm not fond of town life," Lord Rowan said amiably. "That nonsense and mummery never appealed to me. I hired a house every spring when Lady Rowan was alive, and I did my duty by Emily and Louisa, but nowadays when I must take my seat in the Upper House, I stay at a hotel. Our Beryl takes after me; she prefers the country life. Don't you, puss?"

His younger daughter nodded as she helped herself to the veal cutlets.

Lord Rowan was in his late fifties. The impact of his presence was partly due to his size and splendid physique, but was also the product of a forceful personality, a booming voice, and his hearty laugh. Passionately devoted to his children, his horses, his dogs, his pigs, and his land, he was enormously proud of his lineage and heritage. A collection of contradictions, his lordship claimed to detest all persons of the middle class yet maintained cordial relations with his own tenantry and laborers. Always in need of a task on which to expend a measure of his overabundant energy, he was happy to assist the estate workers with mending a hedge or felling a tree.

"Have you never been to London, Lady Beryl?" Damon asked.

"When I was twelve I went to a school in Hans Place," she said. "Briefly."

A low, rumbling chuckle rolled up from the earl's broad chest. "My puss missed Deerhurst, and soon came home to us—but only after she'd offended the headmistress by adopting one stray mongrel, two kittens, and a score of attic mice."

"What happened to the menagerie?" Damon inquired.

Eyes dancing, she replied, "The mongrel and the cats are now well up in years, and you'll find them nosing about the kitchen, on the lookout for a morsel from the staff. The mice preferred to stay behind in Hans Place."

Louisa shook her head, and for the second time that day bemoaned the fact that her sister had never enjoyed a proper London season. "I shall never forget my own. Do you remember the year I made my come-out, Damon?"

"How could I forget? I was pressed into service as your dancing partner, along with Sid and John, by my cousin Roger, who wanted to prevent the smart town beaux from monopolizing you."

"The wretch! He never told me that!"

Smiling, Damon dredged up another old memory. "Do you recall the red satin waistcoat with the gold embroidery John was sporting at your ball?"

From his end of the table, the earl thundered, "Lord, yes, and a regular popinjay he looked!"

"He was so proud of it," Louisa sighed. "Dear John, how we miss him."

Damon tactfully eased into another, less distressing reflection of years gone by. He, too, missed the Honorable John Kinnard, who had fallen at Barrosa, but counted the family fortunate: of the three sons who had gone off to the wars, only one had been lost.

After the tablecloth was removed, the ladies left the gentlemen to their port and political talk and withdrew to the room across the hall. Beryl sat down before the pianoforte in the alcove to examine a book of music. As Louisa straightened the contents of her sewing box, her discourse centered on the loved ones she had left at Fairdown.

Within the hour the gentlemen joined them, the earl taking the chair nearest the instrument, and when he requested a favorite air, his daughter obliged him. It was a simple country tune, vaguely familiar to Damon from his youth. Lady Beryl's proficiency was far greater than he had expected, and her clear soprano was complemented by her father's deep bass. After several songs, Louisa rang for tea. It was a yawning Cedric who broke up the party, and everyone followed him into the dim hall, lit only by the bedroom candles waiting on a marble-topped console table at the foot of the great staircase.

As her father and brother went up to their respective chambers, Louisa pulled Damon aside and confided, "Your coming to stay is a wonderful thing. I'm so happy I thought of it! Papa needs a diversion as much as Beryl, I think, and fortunately he's on his best behavior. Why, last night when she played and sang, he was looking so mournful that it nearly broke my heart. Honestly, I don't know which is worse, his bearish mood or his despairing one!" As they approached the foot of the stairs, she fell silent in the manner of one who does not wish to be overheard.

Beryl handed her sister a lit taper, then gave another to Damon. With a shrewdness he considered most unbecoming, she said, "If your lordship remains with us a week, *I* shall be much surprised."

Before he could answer, she took up the remaining candle from the table and began to ascend the staircase swiftly and without a backward glance.

# 2

*Tell of towns storm'd, of Armies over-run*
*And mighty kingdoms by your conduct won.*
—EDMUND WALLER

Like the other members of her family, Beryl had
a sunny disposition, but she was also sensitive
enough to be troubled by Lord Elston's disapproval. His failure to remember her was also
wounding, although she knew she had been eminently forgettable at age twelve, small and thin,
her hair always in a tangle. She had noticed him,
though, for in her dazzled eyes, her brothers' dashing friend had been the epitome of masculine re-
finement and sophistication, and she had fancied
herself in love. Only when he began flirting with
Miss Honoria Capshaw, the toast of the neighborhood, had Beryl accepted the futility of her longings.

Thus far his lordship's behavior was consistent
with the past, if not worse. During a solitary
breakfast she considered his conduct of the night
before and decided being ignored was preferable
to being frowned upon.

She looked up from her assault upon her egg
cup when the subject of her reverie entered the
dining room. He wore the modest garb of a gentleman bent upon rustication, buckskins and riding

boots, and only the intricate design of his cravat
and the cut-steel buttons of his brown coat be-
spoke him the man of fashion. Surprised that he'd
elected to keep country hours, she said, "I'm
afraid we must dine *à deux*, as Ceddie seldom stirs
before noon, and my father has left for the Home
Farm. He visits his pigs first thing every morning."

"Is Louisa a late riser?" Damon asked, taking a
seat.

"Oh, no. For the last hour she has been bustling
about the house, wearing a very *conscious* look. I
daresay it's because Roger and the boys will be
visiting her today. Oh, don't bother with that
bacon; it must be stone-cold. Jessom, please bring
more of it for his lordship—and muffins for me."

The butler soon returned with the requested additions to a table already laden with food. As
Damon filled his plate, he asked, "And how do you
occupy yourself during the day, Lady Beryl?"

"I ride in the morning, when the weather permits, and in the afternoon I work in my garden
or practice my music, or read. I'm like Papa in
preferring outdoor pursuits, but unlike him, I'm
also fond of books."

A constrained silence fell, only to be broken by
the earl calling to his daughter from outside the
house. Beryl dropped her fork and jumped out of
her chair, rushing to the window.

Lord Rowan, astride his heavy-boned roan stal-
lion, was below. "Landor has dug up a baby
hedgehog," he informed her, his voice muffled by
the glass. "D'you want it?"

"You know I do," she answered. "Where is he?"

"My coat pocket. Open the window and I'll hand
him up, but mind you don't tumble out and break
your head!" When she leaned out, he rose up in

the stirrups to place a smell gray lump into her cupped hands. "I suppose he can take the place of that damned squirrel," he said gruffly, and with a flourish of his whip, he was off.

Beryl emerged from the window and went to show off her prize to Damon. "Would you like to hold him?"

"Thank you, no. It's very young. How shall you raise it?"

She smoothed the silver-tipped spines and said, "I'll ask the gardeners to save some snails. And he'll have to get used to eating hen's eggs, because our gamekeeper will never agree to provide him with pheasant or partridge eggs!" Her new pet lifted its head to sniff about curiously, and she laughed. "I always wanted a hedgehog. Ceddie will be so jealous! When I had my tame squirrel he was mad to have one too, and was quite as distraught as I when Master Nuts caught a fatal inflammation of the lungs. He could run up and down your arms and across your shoulders, and I very nearly taught him to play the pianoforte— the squirrel, that is, not Ceddie."

Damon, reaching for a piece of toast, remarked dryly, "So talented a fellow must be sorely missed."

"I think," she said thoughtfully, "I had better give this little fuzzypig to my nephews before I grow too much attached to him. They can better give him the attention he deserves. I'd give him a name, though, if only I could think of something suitable."

"Rupert," said her table companion without hesitation. "A friend of mine bears a striking resemblance to your friend there. Pointy nose, no chin, small dark eyes. Everyone called him Hedgehog."

Beryl, still stroking the newly christened Rupert, asked Damon by what nickname he had been called during his schooldays.

"I forget," he replied curtly.

She glanced over at him and saw that he was looking grim. "Was it so very dreadful?"

"It seemed so at the time."

"I expect it had something to do with the tale of Damon and Pythias," she hazarded.

"Nothing so creditable. I was never as popular as your brothers."

"John and Sid and Tracy liked you very well," she said.

"We grew up together. Fairdown was once my home, and Deerhurst nearly so."

His parents, she knew, had been involved in some scandal. Though they had not divorced, they lived apart for many years before dying together in a carriage accident. It occurred to her that the aloof, self-contained gentleman must have been a very lonely little boy. Beryl, who had always been cossetted and treasured by her family, could not imagine a life bereft of loving parents, gentle sisters, and lively brothers to play with and to plague.

Tenderly gathering her pet to her breast, she abandoned the uncommunicative marquis to his breakfast and the Portsmouth newspaper, which he was eyeing covetously.

As soon as she was gone, Damon set down his fork and reached for the newssheet, but the list of ships in port failed to excite his interest and the only news from London was political, not social. Bored, and with no prospect of being anything else for some time, he left the dining parlor, wondering where Lady Beryl had run off to.

He supposed she was really no worse than the

most graceless of the girls he met—and shunned—
at the assemblies in town. But her free and easy
manners were deplorable, and he did not condone
her cradling a hedgehog at the breakfast table.
Lord Rowan had better let her marry that young
commoner, he thought, for she was not likely to
attract a gentleman of title.

He whiled away the rest of the morning in the
library, writing letters to people he didn't even
like and had not, in his wildest imaginings, expected to miss. He was wondering how long it
would be before he went to Louisa with some
plausible excuse for his necessary and immediate
return to town when Cedric challenged him to a
game of billiards.

They were so occupied when a pair of children
burst into the room. "Hullo, Jack," Cedric greeted
the elder one. "What's that you've got?"

"Rupert," the boy replied, looking down at the
small creature peeping out from the pocket of his
jacket. "Auntie Beryl gave him me." Master Jack
Meriden, aged six, eyed the tall blond gentleman
curiously, as did brother Harry, three years his
junior.

"This is your Cousin Damon," Cedric announced
unceremoniously. "Now be off, rascals—you know
Papa doesn't want you in this room."

Harry cowered at the mention of his formidable
grandsire, but Jack said staunchly, "We're hiding."

"Well, you can't do it here," his uncle retorted,
leaning across the table to aim his shot, and the
children vanished.

The game was soon interrupted again by Beryl,
who asked, "Have you seen Jack and Harry? I've
been looking all over."

"I just chased 'em away," her brother replied.

"Oh, dear." She nodded at Damon. "Roger is asking for you—he's with Louisa. Will you come?"

He went with her to the drawing room, where they found Sir Roger Meriden and his lady sitting together on the sofa. Louisa, her face flushed, said gaily, "You must hear my happy news—now that I've told Roger, there's no harm in making it generally known. I shall be lying-in again before Christmas!"

While Damon offered his felicitations on the happy expectation of another little Meriden, Beryl embraced her sister. Then, smiling fondly upon her brother-in-law, a pleasant-faced gentleman with chestnut hair, she said, "Dear Roger, I do hope you'll have a daughter this time! My nephews are delightful, but the older I get the more appealing is the prospect of a quiet, well-behaved girl. Sewing samplers and dressing dolls with her will seem so restful after taking part in Jack and Harry's pursuits!"

"You were never one to so occupy yourself," the baronet reminded her, "for I seldom saw you with sampler in hand. You, Beryl, are living proof that not every little girl is a model of propriety."

When he tweaked one of her brown curls, she gave him a saucy look. "Haven't you forgiven me for upsetting the ink bottle onto your best breeches? That was all of ten years ago!"

With a pained expression, Sir Roger replied, "No, nor have I forgotten the day you borrowed my horse without permission. Or the frightful pair of slippers you embroidered for my birthday, or how you wept when I wouldn't wear them in company. I was in a quake for fear Louisa would make me do so, lest you fall into a fever from disappointment!"

"Enough!" Beryl cried, putting her hands to her ears. "Someday, when my past offenses are repeated by your daughter, you'll point me out as the very pinnacle of perfection!" After advising Damon not to believe a word, she added, "Roger has traduced my character most thoroughly, but there's not a breath of truth in him. Poor man, he grows forgetful with his advancing age!"

The baronet and his lady laughed at this speech. Damon did not.

As soon as the men left for the stableyard, Beryl joined her sister on the sofa. "You'll be wanting to return to Fairdown."

"Are you mad?" Louisa replied. "I should be worn to death at home, for Roger always becomes overly solicitous when I'm increasing. No, I prefer to remain at Deerhurst. I can depend on seeing him often; he says the distance is perfect exercise for his horses, the rogue. Besides, even if I hadn't set my heart upon a house-party, I couldn't leave you unchaperoned with Damon in the house."

"Why not?" Beryl asked. "Papa and Ceddie are here."

"Oh, but you must have a woman. Not that I have any concerns," Louisa declared, "but people might talk, which would be unpleasant for you both."

Beryl said thoughtfully, "I suppose you're right."

"It's no great sacrifice, my being here, and I confess I'm rather enjoying this little holiday."

"You make a very poor case for matrimony," murmured Beryl. But even as she tried to smile, she felt the sharp stab of envy.

Louisa took one limp hand and squeezed it comfortingly. "Oh, my dear, don't despair! I feel sure that Papa will come 'round in time."

As Beryl returned the pressure of Louisa's fingers, she made every effort to look hopeful, but she wondered if her overly protective parent would ever accept her marriage with complaisance.

When another two days passed with no news of an Army transport ship reaching Portsmouth, the Kinnards' collective impatience knew no bounds.

On Lord Elston's fourth night at Deerhurst, the family sat together as usual in the drawing room, trying to conceal their disappointment. Cedric sat in a corner, his nose in a book, while Damon and Louisa played piquet, with desultory exchanges of gossip after each game. Lord Rowan and Beryl waged war at the chessboard, their eyes fixed upon the squares and the positions of each piece.

The brown and white spaniel reposing at the young lady's feet, the first to hear the crunch of carriage wheels, let out a sharp bark.

"Be silent, Gypsy!" Beryl commanded. "Oh, Papa, do you think—can it possibly be—"

In an instant the Kinnards were on their feet. They rushed into the great hall, the excited dog chasing after them and Damon bringing up the rear. At the door a damp-eyed Jessom attended to a pair of uniformed gentlemen, one wearing the red coat of a staff officer, the other in the blue of a hussar regiment.

Beryl hurled herself at the taller of the two, whose left arm was cradled in a sling. "Sidney! Oh, Sid!" she cried, as he encircled her with his sound limb and hugged her close. Breathless with mingled tears and laughter, she begged him to release her. "You'll hurt your poor arm, and I must hug Tracy!" Turning to the other soldier, who was slender and fine-boned, she said unevenly, "Welcome home."

He was less demonstrative than his brother, and merely kissed her cheek. "This is a fine way to greet a lieutenant, little squirrel, weeping all over his regimentals. A little more respect, if you please!"

Meanwhile, Sidney had swept Louisa into his one-armed embrace. "Oh, Sid," said that lady worriedly, "you must take care. Does your wound pain you very much?"

"Not tonight," he assured her. "Only let me have another go at Beryl and I'll be fine, for hers is the best medicine in the world. Would that we could take her back to the lads in the Peninsula!"

Beryl raised shining eyes from her rapt inspection of Tracy's gold-braided shako. "And shouldn't I love to follow the drum! You must be mending very quickly, Sid, for you've managed to bruise every one of my ribs. I'll take good care to keep out of your way when you regain full use of your arm!"

Captain the Honorable Sidney Kinnard's booming laugh was reminiscent of his father's, and he resembled the earl more completely than any of his siblings. The rigors of the southern campaigns clearly agreed with him: his face was bronzed by the sun and constant activity had muscled his large frame. Tracy, three years younger, was similarly lean and tanned, but he was quieter, more graceful in his movements. Sidney, like their father, was forceful and energetic.

As soon as the conquering heroes were seated in the drawing room, their relations directed a barrage of questions at them. Cedric clamored to know how it felt to take part in a battle, the earl demanded news of the progress of the war, and Louisa offered food and drink. Only Beryl and Damon were silent. She was overpowered by happiness; he was reluctant to intrude upon so intimate a family scene.

Lord Rowan thundered, "When did you fellows arrive, and why the devil didn't you send word the moment you docked?"

"We thought the surprise too rich to pass up," Sidney answered. He looked up at his hovering sister and said, "No, Louisa, we aren't a bit hungry. We ate our dinner at Portsmouth. But some brandy wouldn't go amiss. I say, Papa, do you still receive French goods in the night?"

"Aye," said his father curtly. "But if you're thinking to harangue at me for keeping smuggled spirits, or anything else the Gentlemen choose to leave on my property, you can save your breath. It's the way of things along the coast, and well you know it!"

Tracy Kinnard frowned. "That may be so, sir, but your support of the free trade supplies the very muskets the French use against us."

Lord Rowan, disliking criticism from his children, bellowed, "Nonsense! I'm supporting the local men, Rowley and the others, not the blasted Frogs!"

Beryl, pouring the amber liquid from the decanter, begged them not to quarrel.

Despite his acid comment, Tracy accepted a glass from her and said, "The squirrel has grown into a young lady since we left for the wars, Sid."

"When I last saw you, Beryl, you were all arms and legs and a mop of tousled hair. Five years have wrought a prodigious change!" Sidney glanced at Damon. "And what might you be doing here, my friend? Grown tired of London at last?"

Damon looked up from stroking the sleepy spaniel to find six pairs of Kinnard eyes upon him. "You rate your charms too low. When I heard of your imminent return, I simply couldn't keep away."

Cedric broke in upon the laughter to say, "Beryl, you haven't told Sid and Tracy about Mr. Yeates."

Conscious of a tension that had been absent a moment before, Sidney asked, "And who is Mr. Yeates?"

"Our Beryl is engaged to be married," Louisa said calmly, ignoring her father's menacing frown.

"She most certainly is not, nor will she ever be," Lord Rowan contradicted her. "I don't approve of the match, so we may cease to think and talk of it!"

Sidney and Tracy exchanged amused smiles at their parent's belief that he had the power to direct the thoughts of his family.

As Damon hastily threw himself into the breach and guided the conversation into less controversial channels, a white-faced Beryl retreated to the alcove. Her father's harsh words had shocked and angered her, and inwardly she railed at his unjust rejection of the young man she hadn't seen since leaving Yorkshire.

Initially her acquaintance with Peter had been social, the result of standing up together at one of the York Assemblies during the winter. He was a pleasant, personable young man with blond hair and soulful brown eyes, and his attentions had grown more and more particular with the passing weeks. Never before had anyone set out to win her affections, and she was entirely susceptible to his wooing. He had proposed during an afternoon stroll on the grounds.

"But you really must ask Papa's permission," she had told her suitor. "He's quite old-fashioned about such things, though I know he'll be happy for me—we are devoted to one another. I believe he's in London just now, at Nerot's Hotel."

Peter had agreed to speak to the earl at once, and before leaving Yorkshire he promised to meet Beryl at Deerhurst within a fortnight.

Little had she guessed that the fortnight might stretch into a month, or that Papa, rather than inviting his future son-in-law down to Sussex, would return from London quite alone and most unwilling to discuss what had passed between them. Beryl, who had no very clear notion of her intended's fortune, much less any idea of what marriage portion she would receive, had asked him outright.

"Don't go pestering me with questions, puss, it's not maidenly," he had replied in his most abrupt fashion. "Time enough to be thinking of weddings, for you're young yet and have little knowledge of the world."

"I'm twenty-two, Papa."

"You've only known the fellow three months, at most."

"Neither did you know Mama very long before you were wed," she had pointed out. "And how will I ever know Mr. Yeates better if we remain apart?"

The earl eyed his small but formidable daughter warily. "You can't make an unequal match, puss. They rarely prosper."

"I don't expect you to rejoice over his lineage, Papa, but even you must admit Peter cannot help who his grandfather is. Besides, he was raised a gentleman, and if you are looking higher than that for my husband, I assure you I am not!"

He grunted and said vaguely, "Well, perhaps we'll ask him down here in the autumn. He does hunt, doesn't he?"

Beryl couldn't say, and wondered if she would ever be permitted to find out, for her betrothal remained a closed subject. And her experience of her parent's volatile moods warned her that to plague him would be disastrous.

But the resulting rift had alarmed her. Cognizant of her own faults—impulsiveness being the primary one—she was naturally reluctant to appear anything less than a paragon in her doting father's eyes. Theirs had been a special closeness, bound as they were by a shared love of outdoor pursuits, all living creatures, most growing things, and music. If she hadn't met Peter Yeates, she would have been content to remain at his side forever. Now she was torn between loyalty to the one who had always been her best friend and chief admirer, and her new love for the compelling young man who had touched her untried heart.

Because her father had never denied her anything for very long, she shared Louisa's expectation that in time he would relent. At first she had not doubted Peter's constancy, but now that he moved in a larger sphere, she was growing concerned. His recent letter had announced his intention of remaining fixed in London for the present, and he'd hinted that he might visit Brighton later in the summer. Beryl could well imagine the crop of enchanting creatures he would meet at the assemblies in town and also at the fashionable seaside resort, girls who were younger and prettier than she, and more lavishly dowered. Would he continue to think her delightful, enchanting, a darling—all those gratifying things he had whispered to her when they had parted? She tried to shove these fears to the back of her mind whenever they obtruded, but was not always successful.

Her siblings were proving as much a trial to her as her father's stubbornness. First Cedric had made her an object of close study, then Louisa had descended on Deerhurst to press their parent into accepting the betrothal. These intrusions into her customary routine made her feel like one of the handsome swans on the lake at Petworth, gliding through life forever watched and exclaimed over, an object of fascination to those around her. Cedric's inquisitiveness was worse than Louisa's constant attempts to cheer her, for he had the habit of asking extremely personal questions in order to depict his heroine's feelings accurately. She gave candid answers, for it was not her nature to dissemble. She hoped his novel-writing experiment would last no longer than had his intention to walk the length of England last summer. He had started at Selsey Bill, but upon reaching Chichester had met an acquaintance; after a convivial hour at a tavern, the two young men had visited a horse auction in the neighborhood. Cedric had surprised his family by turning up at Deerhurst for dinner, and they never heard anything more of his walking tour.

Sidney's voice intruded upon her thoughts. "If you play for us, little sister, I'll turn the pages for you."

Sitting down at the pianoforte, Beryl wondered if a united front might sway their father. Of the two soldiers, it was Sidney who had the most influence with him.

Under the cover of a sonata she whispered, "Sid, I must speak with you, in private."

"When and where?" he asked, his voice a conspiratorial murmur.

"The kitchen garden, tomorrow morning."

"Ten o'clock?"

She nodded, missing a note.

When Beryl finished, everyone applauded but Louisa, who announced, "I've just had a most wonderful idea! We must have one of our musical evenings. A concert would be the perfect entertainment for the guests."

"By Jupiter, so it would!" Cedric cried.

"I'll be no use to you," said Sidney, shrugging his sound shoulder. "It's hard to play the fiddle with but one good arm."

Beryl said sunnily, "Perhaps not, but you can serve as my page-turner as you have done so splendidly tonight." She looked over at her father to judge his reaction. "What say you, Papa? Have we your permission?"

"It would be like old times," the earl replied. "We've not played for company since your mother died, nor all of us together for many a year."

Cedric, seeing that Damon looked bemused, strove to enlighten him. "We had a family orchestra. We all play instruments."

"Not I," Louisa disclaimed. "I haven't a scrap of talent. The rest are creditable musicians, though, especially Beryl."

"You'll be sadly rusty, Tracy," Cedric said with a triumphant smile at his senior.

"He will practice," Beryl said. "As will all of us—just as Herr Mann would wish. 'Practice, prac-

tice, *kinder, und* you will be all as *gut* as the earl
and his so *gnädige* lady!' " Her mimicry of their
music master amused her siblings, and even Lord
Rowan let out a loud guffaw, startling the somno-
lent spaniel.

It was agreed that the musical members of the
group would undertake the project, and when the
issue was decided Tracy raised the obvious question of what piece they ought to play. Beryl, with
a decisiveness he likened to that of a field marshal,
ordered him to the music room to collect some
music, and when he returned, the young people
pored over the pages, passing them back and
forth.

"What about this bit of Bach?" Damon held up
a stack loosely tied with a faded ribbon. "It's the
Concerto in D."

Beryl took it from him. "Oh, I do like Bach! But
can we fill all the parts? How many are we?"

"Four," answered Tracy and Cedric together.

She shook her head regretfully. "That's barely
half the number we'd need."

Damon lifted his head and said, "I hesitate to
mention it amongst so many *virtuosi*, but I do play
the violin myself." When Beryl's eyes widened
with new respect, he amended, "Somewhat indif-
ferently, I fear, but if you require another string I
am at your service."

"But we'll still be short," Cedric commented.

Smiling triumphantly, Beryl cried, "I know! We
must ask Herr Mann to come to us. I'm sure he
will; he lived at Deerhurst forever, and Papa was
his first patron. May we send for him?" she asked,
once more deferring to her parent.

"As you wish, puss. Music is my chief delight,"
the earl confessed to Damon, "apart from my gar-

dens. Many a winter night Lady Rowan and I would play together, and as the children came, our orchestra grew."

Beryl, after toting up numbers on her fingers, nodded in satisfaction. "Herr Mann can conduct and take the first violin, and now we have another in Cousin Damon. I'll play the harpsichord, Ceddie the flute, Papa the viola, Tracy the cello. What else?"

She looked at Damon expectantly, and he carried the music over to one of the sconces and submitted them to a thorough review. Soon he reported, "One more viola. A violin. The bass viol."

"Must we send for Tom, then?" the earl asked gloomily, referring to his heir. "He's poor company, and I don't much fancy having that wife of his about the place."

"No, no," Beryl assured him, "Herr Mann can bring the necessary players to round out our numbers."

"Doesn't the doctor play bass viol?" Cedric asked.

"To be sure," Louisa answered from her corner. "He played for the dance at the Capshaws' last month. I know he would help you, Beryl. Ever since we called him in last autumn to tend to your sprained shoulder, he's been besotted."

"*Another* admirer?" Sidney quizzed his little sister.

"She has dozens," Cedric informed him. "Not only Dr. Shenstone, but that curate from Chichester, and Giles Capshaw—*and* Bob Rowley."

"Don't be so silly," Beryl said loftily. "Ceddie is sure to be a famous author someday; he has such a wealth of imagination!"

The Kinnards and their guest discussed the concert until bedtime; everyone groaned over the length of the piece and the difficulty of its parts. The gentlemen unanimously voted Beryl concert mistress until Herr Mann should arrive, instantly regretting it when she promised to be very strict with them.

When Damon retired that evening, he was resigned to a longer stay in Sussex than he had originally intended, but he no longer mourned his continued absence from town. No one could be dull with Sidney and Tracy about, and Louisa was counting on him to help her arrange her party. The attractions of Deerhurst were many, and the greatest of them, he had decided, was the very person he'd disliked so intently upon his arrival.

# 3

*Fresh and young, and fair and wise,*
*The worship'd idol of her father's eyes.*
                              —JOHN DRYDEN

At ten o'clock the following morning, Beryl crept into the brick-enclosed kitchen garden. At that hour the sole beneficiaries of nature's bounty were the bees, hard at work and humming busily. She passed rows of peas and parsnips and plots of fragrant herbs, pausing to pluck a blooming columbine which she carried with her to the bench along the wall. Waving it back and forth, she sat down to await Sidney.

Thus far, she reflected, patience had availed her nothing, and when she considered the prospect of a long, lonely summer of watching for the postbag, the circles she traced in the air grew ever more frantic. Several more minutes dragged by, during which she wondered if her brother had forgotten their appointment, but eventually she was rewarded by the sight of his figure striding toward her.

He halted and struck an attitude, placing his good hand over his heart. "What a charming sight—no, don't move an inch, but stay as you are and let me drink you in. I've become so used to the dark Spanish beauties that I'd near forgotten how refreshing a pink English rose can be!"

"Flatterer," she replied affectionately.

"And now you've become a veritable Circe, turning all the local fellows into swine."

"You mustn't listen to Ceddie's foolishness. By now you must also have heard I'm the heroine of his romance—me, of all people! With my ordinary brown hair, and silly snub nose! Stop laughing, you beast."

"But you've got perfect teeth. Before I went to the Peninsula, I underestimated their importance. The Spaniards, most of 'em, are comely enough in their fashion, until they smile."

"I'll be bound they smile at you often enough," Beryl teased. "Why are you so tardy?"

"I've been with Tracy and Papa this half-hour," he informed her. "My comrade-in-arms is selling out to turn gentleman farmer now that old Samuel Tracy, his godfather, has deeded him a snug little property in Kent. Our brother is naturally delighted, but he's such a saint and martyr he worried that Papa would think him derelict in his duty, leaving the Army with the war still going so hot and heavy."

"But he has served for four years, and was wounded. Twice," she added staunchly.

"Papa's only objection seems to be that he can no longer boast of his son the hussar, but I managed to calm him with the reminder that he still has a son on Wellington's staff. I'm no beau, nor so graceful a dancer as Tracy, but my soldiering has certainly recommended me to our commander. And Kinnards are known to be the finest of officers."

"Indeed," his sister agreed, "and they are equally

renowned for their modesty!" He laughed at that, and when his mirth subsided she said thoughtfully, "Tracy was never so devoted to the military life as you and John. I wondered why he allowed Papa to purchase his commission, but Richard says only God knows the workings of Tracy's mind, so we mere mortals will always be confounded by him."

"That sounds like Parson Dick," Sidney said with a grin.

"Now that he has an income, Tracy can marry," she sighed, unhappily aware of her own problems in that respect. "He has loved Honoria Capshaw forever."

Her pensive tone was not lost on the perceptive Sidney, who said, "But what of your prospects, Miss Glum? Come now, tell your brother all about this merchant prince of yours."

Beryl explained in great detail how her friendship with Peter Yeates had developed into much more, bemoaning their father's refusal and his complete disregard for the convention of inviting her suitor to Deerhurst. Spreading her hands helplessly, she concluded, "So you see how uncomfortably I am placed. I hate to hurt Papa, but neither can I forever permit him to undermine my future. Great-aunt Sophia might be senile, but she likes Peter and would support us, as would Louisa. I'm of age; I could easily bolt to London and be married there."

"That must be Papa's greatest fear. You know it would break his heart."

"And mine," she confessed sadly. "If he cast me off, or refused to accept my marriage, I know I'd never be completely happy. But if only he would relent, permit me to see Mr. Yeates again, and become better acquainted with him himself, I'm positive he would cease to look on the match with disfavor."

Sidney turned his head to observe her narrowly. "But you said Papa met Yeates, up in London. Perhaps it's the man he objects to, not only the merchant."

"Peter is a gentleman!" she flashed back. "Papa speaks of him as though he were a clerk in a shop, but it's naught but that old, stupid prejudice talking." She rose and began pacing the garden path, her brow wrinkled in frustration.

Sidney said bracingly, "Never fear, I'll stand your friend—so long as you don't do anything foolish, like plot clandestine meetings, or an elopement."

"Oh, no, I couldn't do that, even if I dared. Peter is fixed in London for the season, and afterward he'll go to Brighton."

"Curse this arm of mine!" he said heatedly. "The doctors expect me to act the invalid, the damned fools, and if I were seen jauntering about in London or Brighton—well, it wouldn't exactly ruin my career, but it wouldn't be wise."

"What about Tracy? Though I hate to tear him away from Honoria when he has only just returned."·

"I think we might persuade him to leave her side for a little while, in support of a worthy cause. I'll speak to him."

Beryl hugged him, taking care not to disturb the injured limb. "You are a darling brother, a paragon amongst men, and the greatest comfort to me! But not a word to Louisa and Ceddie, if you please. They are kind, but . . . oh, you know!"

Sidney, knowing only too well, patted her shoulder in silent sympathy. Though a veteran of many a violent struggle in the Peninsula, he wondered if he possessed the fortitude to enter into the great contest of wills which was turning Deerhurst into a battlefield.

Beryl returned to the house by way of the stableyard, where a horse and gig stood in readiness. When she went inside she met Tracy in the hall, drawing on his gloves in an uncustomarily reckless fashion, and asked, "Where are you off to, Lieutenant Kinnard?"

"To call on Mr. Capshaw and beg his permission to address Honoria. I did so four years ago, before going off to the wars, only to be scolded for my presumption. I'm the same man I ever was, but certainly my prospects are much improved and, I trust, more acceptable."

Beryl reached up to smooth the lapels of his coat. "Dear cynic! You are not nervous, surely?"

"Not nervous? What I feel could more rightly be termed panic! I had rather face old Soult's troops again, or storm Badajoz, than visit our neighbor this morning."

Although she laughed at his dismay, tears were very near the surface. With complete disregard for his elegant dress, she flung her arms around him. "Be happy, Tracy," she whispered. "You and Honoria are so very fortunate!"

He bestowed a careless kiss upon her brow, then walked out into the sunshine.

Beryl's tremulous smile faded and she turned blindly toward the staircase. By the time she reached the half-landing, she was fumbling in the pocket of her gown for her handkerchief. The thud of footsteps warned her someone was coming down, and through a misty blur of tears she perceived Lord Elston. He gazed back at her curiously. "Tracy is to be married," she blurted, before losing control.

With great presence of mind, Damon took Beryl by the arm and drew her into the Long Gallery. He sat her down in a chair, and when her tiny scrap of linen and lace was thoroughly damp he presented his own more substantial handkerchief.

"Thank you," she choked.

"Why does Tracy's engagement reduce you to this sad state?" he asked calmly. "Have you not enough brothers to give one up without a qualm?"

"It isn't that," she said, blotting her cheeks. "I know it's stupid and completely childish, but I envy him so."

"Yes, that is understandable." She looked at him, startled by his dejected tone, and he shook his head. "No, I don't have designs upon the exquisite Miss Capshaw, if that's what you're thinking."

Beryl reached out and placed her hand on his sleeve. "Have you also been thwarted of your heart's desire?"

When Damon's eyes met her damp ones, they hardened, and he answered curtly, "I am not your fellow sufferer. I seek no wife, nor do I envy those who are so eager to leap into matrimony. In fact, Lady Beryl, I pity them with all my heart." He rose abruptly, and after a curt bow, he left her alone.

Beryl, utterly perplexed, clutched his handkerchief. For a moment he had shown how agreeable and sympathetic he could be, then he had suddenly reverted to the chilly disapproval that so distressed her. Wondering what she had said to drive him away, she subjected her own part of their brief dialogue to a careful and thorough review, and her greater troubles were overshadowed by the sorrow of knowing herself an object of pity to Lord Elston.

In the afternoon Beryl went to the library in search of a book and found her sister and Damon there, discussing the house-party.

"It has occurred to me," Louisa was saying, "that we might give a grand ball. Midsummer Night would be ideal, and it could be the most splendid affair the neighborhood has seen for years! I'd want to serve champagne, of course, although the last time I stopped at the vintner's in Chichester, it was hideously expensive. Perhaps there's time enough to arrange matters with the—with the Gentlemen," she concluded primly.

Damon cocked an eyebrow. "Smuggled goods, Louisa?"

Unperturbed, she replied, "Pooh! What's the difference? So long as Tracy doesn't discover, although I'm sure I don't know how he expects us to provide the brandy he likes so much with an embargo against French goods."

Beryl turned from the bookshelves to say, "Bob Rowley told me to let him know if we ever wanted anything particular."

"Then please tell him I need some champagne by mid-month. Such a pity it can't be your betrothal ball, my love."

Conscious of Lord Elston's critical eye, Beryl bit her lower lip and looked away.

Their cabal was interrupted by Lord Rowan, who came in search of their guest, saying, "I'm off to the North Meadow, and then to the village, if you wish to ride." With an apologetic smile at

Louisa, Damon rose. The earl, turning to his daughter, asked if she cared to see the lambs.

Beryl hesitated, but the custom of many years won out over her present grudge against him, and she accepted the invitation. "But I must change into my riding dress."

"You've ten minutes and no more," he called after her retreating figure.

"Why," Louisa asked him, "must you be so fierce, sir, when we all know perfectly well that you'll wait for her? And do stop pacing, I beg you, for you quite ruin my concentration."

"Daughters!" the earl muttered. He continued to roam about the room restlessly, tapping his boots with his whip.

Louisa frowned. "I don't know how Beryl expects you to practice for this concert, Papa, when you can scarcely bear to be indoors. By the way," she went on, easing into the particular subject she wished to discuss with him, "we've formed the intention of giving a ball. For Beryl," she added shrewdly.

"If Beryl wants a ball, she may have it. But mind, Louisa, I'll send you back to Fairdown if you invite that fellow Yeates. I won't have him here. Is that understood?" Lord Rowan crossed to the fireplace and snapped his crop menacingly against the empty grate.

"There's no cause to bluster," murmured Louisa, reaching for her quill to strike the offending name from her list.

Beryl soon returned, wearing a gray riding costume and a hat adorned with a tired-looking feather. Louisa deplored her choice, but Beryl excused it to Damon by saying, "I can't bring myself to wear the fashionable blue habit she gave me last Christmas. I always worry about doing it some great harm, and my ride becomes an ordeal, not a pleasure."

The earl made sure the girth of Beryl's sidesaddle was securely fastened before he tossed her up, and he helped her find the stirrup-iron and adjust her reins as if she were a novice. Meanwhile, Damon was introducing himself to the black horse allotted to him, and in a few minutes the threesome left the stableyard, riding toward a fallow field that adjoined the park.

The spirited little mare sidled and flirted with Damon's hack, and her equally spirited mistress declared, "Sally needs a gallop. She's done nothing but eat for the past two days, and Smith never lets her have her head when he exercises her. I'm itching for a good run myself."

Her father said gruffly, "Suit yourself, then. I must consult with the shepherds about my ewes, and your frolicking will only upset them." But when Beryl set her horse into a canter, he turned to Damon, concern in his eyes, and urged him to go with her. "See that she comes to no harm, and I'll meet you in the village later."

Damon obediently went after the girl and the mare, now tearing through the field at a neck-or-nothing pace. When they reached the tall hedge, Sally curled up her legs and sailed over it. Damon's mount also took the barrier in a flying leap, landing with a thud and a splash on the other side. The animal was sunk in ooze up to his hocks, and Damon's boots and breeches had also suffered.

Beryl, whose laughing face was liberally flecked with mud, gasped, "I *am* sorry! I never guessed what might lie on this side of the hedge." When he reached out to hand her a pristine square of white linen, she said brightly, "Twice in one day! Whatever would I do without you always at hand to press your handkerchief on me?"

Smiling, he said, "I'm the modern equivalent of Sir Walter Raleigh, and my ready handkerchief will accompany the tales of my gallantry down through the years, just as he was famous for spreading his cloak. Wait, you've missed a spot on your chin." He took the cloth from her, saying, "Let me do it."

She raised no objection, but the mare began sidestepping nervously, edging away from him. Concerned that she might bolt, Damon reached for the reins but misjudged the distance, and his hand landed on the young lady's thigh. Flushing, he pulled it away as quickly as if the gray fabric had burned through his tan glove. "Forgive me, Lady Beryl."

"The fault is Sally's," she said, patting the mare's neck in a calming fashion. "Never fear, I'm the last girl in the world to turn missish on you."

They rode on, Damon struggling to quench the spark of excitement ignited by that brief and accidental contact. He had to admire her self-possession, and was equally impressed by her ability to brush off an incident which must have discomfited her. She had astonished him twice, first in failing to resemble the frail, sickly creature of Louisa's letters, and now by proving she was more than the giddy, graceless girl she had sometimes seemed. In fact, he thought as they walked their horses along the lane, she was turning out to be as interesting and unusual as her name.

"How did you come to be called Beryl?" he asked.

"It was Papa's choice. Ridiculous, is it not?"

"It suits you."

"The sad truth is that my parents never dreamed I'd be a girl. Six of the eight who preceded me into this world were boys, and they were fast running out of names. Poor Ceddie was christened Cedric Percival Molyneux Kinnard, and I would have been Digby Carlisle Valerian." Beryl made a face. "But I was a daughter, and they were going to call me Mary and be done with it, until Papa announced that my eyes were the color of beryls. No one could persuade him that it was a terrible name, so I am Beryl Caroline."

Damon cast a surreptitious sideways glance at the lady riding beside him. The close fit of her riding dress revealed the curve of her high, full bosom and flattered the straight and slender waist. Giving in to wicked temptation, he said appreciatively, "You are indeed a jewel of your house, Lady Beryl, in person as well as in name."

"You have the quotation wrong," she pointed out prosaically. "Chastity is the jewel of one's house, or so Shakespeare said. Here is the village," she announced, lifting her whip in greeting as a pair of scruffy children with rosy cheeks hurried out of their path. "And there's Papa, wearing his thundercloud look."

They drew up before an inn built of brick and timber. "What a time you've been," the earl grumbled as he assisted Beryl out of the saddle.

His suggestion that they repair to the tavern for some refreshment found favor with Damon. While the two noblemen washed down their bread and cheese with home-brewed ale, Beryl sipped a glass of lemonade and listened absently to her father's praise of his flock and the fecundity of his ewes. When they were done he paid off the tapster, and while thus occupied was accosted by an individual whose blackened face and leather apron proclaimed him the village smith. The two men entered into an amiable conversation about a worrisome plague of young foxes in the neighborhood, and Beryl, knowing from experience that it would not end soon, tugged at Damon's sleeve.

"Look," she said, nodding toward the window, "Dr. Shenstone is coming out of his house. Let's ask if he'll join our orchestra."

Damon noted that the doctor held the young lady's small hand a fraction longer than civility required, and when the other man was presented to him, he was very much aware of the wary glance he received. Although he tried to assume the harmless aspect of a surrogate brother, in fact he regarded the stocky surgeon in an equally measuring way. Dr. Shenstone, it transpired, was delighted by Beryl's invitation.

She promised to send his music, that he might begin to study his part. "Smith will bring it tomorrow. We expect Herr Mann to reach Deerhurst by week's end, when we hope to begin our daily rehearsals."

The doctor, after asking for news of Lady Louisa, wondered if Captain Kinnard's injury required his services, and her ladyship's assurances that the arm was healing very well did not seem to cheer him. He accompanied Beryl and Damon to the innyard, where the ostler informed them that the earl had gone to the smithy and said they should not wait for him.

Damon signaled to the man to bring their

horses. In the absence of Beryl's father, he helped her to mount, and he couldn't quite repress a smile of triumph when they rode away together, leaving the good doctor in a cloud of dust.

# 4

*His face is fair as heav'n*
*When springing buds unfold;*
*O why to him was't giv'n*
*Whose heart is wintry cold?*
—WILLIAM BLAKE

After his ride, a thoughtful Damon returned to Louisa and her ever-present guest list.

"I thought perhaps we should invite your friend Lord Blythe," she said, looking up. "Would he and Lady Blythe come, do you think?"

"Certainly, and might even persuade Justin and his lovely wife to join our revels," Damon replied.

"I've never met Lady Cavender. I believe Roger's Uncle Isaac is fond of her."

"Oh, yes, and takes full credit for making that match, forgetting that I had a hand in it too. I've seldom seen the Cavenders since little Juliet's christening, and as a consequence I'm barely on nodding terms with my only goddaughter."

After reviewing the names she had written, Louisa said mournfully, "Nearly everyone is married, save you, and there's no fun in that for Beryl. What's to be done?"

Damon obligingly suggested a single lady and

gentleman of his acquaintance. "And you might ask my cousin Charlotte," he added.

"It's hardly the sort of fashionable entertainment she's used to. So lively and clever a lady will surely be bored at Deerhurst."

"Oh, Charlotte is ever glad of a chance to escape her mother's clutches, and I wager you any sum you like that if I write her by the next post, she'll be here at week's end." Happy though he would be to see his cousin again, he was prompted more by the necessity of importing a diversion as speedily as possible, lest he become too much interested in Louisa's sister.

As he predicted, Miss Charlotte Selby arrived at Deerhurst within a very few days, accompanied by her French maid. The first member of the family to greet her was Cedric, who welcomed her in a polite but vague fashion and delivered her to Louisa, busy composing menus for the dinners which would precede the concert and ball.

Well above average in height, Charlotte greatly resembled the willowy females in the fashion plates of *Ackermann's Repository* and the *Ladies' Magazine* and was just as modishly attired. Society had long ago decreed that her style and her wit were her primary fascinations, for she was not pretty. Her features were as sharp as her tongue could often be, and her wiry black hair, long nose, and overly pale complexion were not considered assets. A pair of dark eyes was her only claim to beauty.

At dinner she had an opportunity to examine all the Kinnards together, and well before the meal was over she had decided they were a delightful family. Lady Louisa was friendly, the brothers were agreeable, and she perceived at a glance that

Lord Rowan's rough exterior and hearty bluffness
hid a soft heart. Lady Beryl was charming, yet
made no attempt to charm. She might lack the
polish and flair which Charlotte possessed in
abundance, but even without them she had managed to captivate that scamp of a Damon, and just
as obviously neither knew nor cared.

The following day the earl, accompanied by his
sons, attended a horse auction, and Lady Louisa
received a visit from her husband. Charlotte seized
this chance for a private talk with her cousin,
whom she discovered in the library, doing nothing
in particular.

"I'm glad you were able to break free of Cousin
Julia," he told her, rousing himself.

"I, too," she said fervently. "All this season
Mama has been singing the praises of matrimony,
as though she hadn't been widowed for a donkey's
years herself and very well satisfied to be so. She
didn't object my coming here because she has convinced herself that you mean to make me an
offer."

"Oh?"

"Why else would you send for me?" she retorted, and he laughed. "Mama seems not to care
that I've become a wealthy woman in my own
right with no need of you or your riches."

Damon regarded her with interest. "Has someone provided you with some riches of your own?"

"Lady Beatrice Lovell, our great-aunt. You must
have heard that she died? We're only just out of
black gloves."

"No one bothered to tell me. Where in the world
did she acquire money? Every penny of the Lovell
fortune is tied up in me, and I know she wasn't
one of my pensioners."

"It's an odd story. Do you care to hear it?" When he nodded, she said, "Years ago, Aunt Beatrice had a suitor, and being a typical Lovell she chose not to marry him. Her gentleman, constant to the last, died a bachelor and left her all his worldly possessions. I believe his estate originally included property, which she later sold, and some shares. Her man of business managed her investments judiciously, with the result that they now yield an income of three thousand a year. Because Aunt disapproved of females who marry to oblige their families—or who marry at all—she left her money to me."

"Now you'll have a host of fortune hunters to choose from," Damon pointed out.

Charlotte laughed. "My legacy isn't likely to tempt anyone of my present acquaintance to court me." Her black eyes lost some of their fire when she said, "It suits my convenience, having funds of my own, and I'm fast learning that money has a liberating effect."

"Not in my experience," Damon said sourly. A moment later, he placed a hand on his cousin's bony shoulder and said contritely, "I'm sorry, Charlie, but dearly though I love you, I won't be making you an offer."

"I've never expected you to," she answered, smiling up at him.

"Tell your mother I asked and you refused, tell her anything you wish, so long as you make her understand that I will not marry."

"Not me, perhaps," she said slyly.

"Just what do you mean by that?"

"Lately—which is to say within the past twenty-four hours—I've begun to wonder if the right lady might change your mind."

"If you're turning into a romantic," sighed Damon, "I fear for our friendship."

"I accept that you're a superior being, but not that you are immune to the human emotions. Give up that absurd notion that being the son of the infamous Beau Lovell makes any difference."

"I think we'd best change the subject," he said darkly.

"You can't let it rule your life forever," said Charlotte, disregarding his warning. "People may say you are like him, but it's only because of your appearance."

"I may not be so cruel as he was, but I am every bit as faithless. Any lady of my intimate acquaintance will tell you that I have no heart."

"Eliza Preston, for instance? Did you really break with her before you left town?"

"Is that what she says?"

"Mama heard it from one of her friends. She always follows the progress of your amours."

"Then in future I shall do my utmost to keep her well entertained." Damon dropped into the nearest chair, then demanded that she tell him all the London news. "I'm starved for gossip."

She obligingly embarked upon a pithy description of the latest follies of their town friends. Because he was in such a strange, grim mood, she didn't dare broach the subject of his evident preoccupation with Lady Beryl Kinnard.

Charlotte was fonder of Damon than of anyone else she knew. He had danced with her at her very first ball, he'd escorted her to any number of parties, and had been a witty and well dressed companion for many a promenade in Hyde Park. She was acquainted with all of his flirts and cordially detested the majority of his mistresses. And she had never put any faith in the old rumor that he had wanted to marry Lady Miranda Peverel, now the Viscountess Cavender. Charlotte knew better, for his aversion to the wedded state had been fixed long before he left Eton. No female could hold his interest indefinitely, he often declared, and thus far his actions had proved it.

But something other than the summer sun had thawed his arctic smile and icy blue eyes, and his cousin hoped it was Lady Beryl Kinnard.

On the following day a heavy fog rolled inland from the sea. Herr Mann, who had arrived that week with two of his countrymen and three instrument cases, saw to it that the Kinnards made the most of their enforced seclusion. The doctor was sent for, and the musicians began rehearsing in earnest.

Sidney, with nothing else to occupy him, offered to show Miss Selby the portraits in the Long Gallery. Pausing before a miniature painted on ivory, Charlotte commented, "How well the artist has captured Lady Beryl's face, particularly the eyes. She makes a charming subject."

"Yes," he said. "Beryl is our good fairy. She's engaged to a chap from Yorkshire, but our father withholds his consent."

Charlotte was very sorry to learn that the young lady who brought out all of Damon's best and most delightful qualities had a prior attachment. "What is Lord Rowan's objection?"

"Mr. Yeates's grandfather is connected with trade," Sidney explained.

"However did Lady Beryl meet him?"

"They were introduced at the York Assemblies."

Charlotte came to an abrupt halt. "The tradesman had tickets of admission?" she asked in amazement.

Her escort burst into laughter. "York, Miss Selby, not London! The true aristocracy of the North is that of the factories and warehouses, one thing my father is quite unable to accept. It's hard enough for him to face the fact that Beryl, who has never shown a preference for any of the neighbors' sons, wishes to marry a complete stranger. Once it was nothing but teasing and jokes whenever she and Papa were together," he said, wagging his head sadly. "I expect there will be a rift in our family ere long, and my brothers and sisters will take Beryl's side. She has a right to a proper life, and a husband and children."

"A *proper* life?" Charlotte murmured, with a sideways glance. "Not every maiden aspires to matrimony, Captain Kinnard."

"Nor does every gentleman," he shot back. He was conscious of the fact that this sloe-eyed, long-legged, black-haired wench was no ordinary female. Smiling, he said, "I've a sudden fancy to play billiards, Miss Selby. Would you like to try my father's table?"

"What about your arm?"

"Don't tell Louisa, but I began playing yesterday, and am none the worse for it. In all fairness I ought to warn you that, impaired as I am, I've still beaten everyone in the house save Damon."

"He was my instructor," Charlotte answered, a distinct note of challenge in her voice.

Despite the good intentions of all the musicians and the skill of some, the first rehearsal of the Bach concerto was a grave disappointment. Lord Rowan and his children labored over the piece, stifling their complaints when fingers long idle began to ache with weariness. When the portly music master finally lowered his baton, the Kinnards, Lord Elston, and Dr. Shenstone laid their instruments aside with thankful sighs, imbued with the desire to play more creditably next time.

"Ve must verk hard togedder, my lords *und* my lady *und* gentlemen," Herr Mann said as his players dispersed. His twenty years among the more phlegmatic English had not taught him a similar reserve, and he was wildly optimistic and utterly despairing by turns. "Only three veeks to prepare ourselves!" he declared, shaking his head. "You vill see how short is the time to make of this piece perfection, as Herr Bach himself vould vish."

Beryl whispered to Damon that Herr Bach must be turning in his grave in horror at their rendition of his masterpiece, which was all but ruined by missed notes and inconsistent timing.

On Thursday of that week the orchestra temporarily disbanded to attend the King's birthday fête. The village of Rowan was determined to celebrate the seventy-fourth anniversary of His Majesty's birth as though he still ruled over them. The people were glad of any excuse for festivity, in the absence of good tidings from London. Mr. Spencer Perceval, the prime minister, had been assassinated the previous month, precipitating a government crisis. The Prince Regent was emptying the nation's coffers to pay for the lavish improvements to his various residences. News from the Peninsula was indefinite, and for every victory reported there was always a defeat.

So on the fourth of June the Kinnards and their guests, along with the rest of the village, stood on the green, cheering the half-dozen lads who ran in the foot-race, and the earl presented the prize himself.

The winner was a lanky, shaggy-haired young man, a former playmate of Beryl's, and she hurried to his side to offer congratulations. "You are still the fleetest fellow in the parish, Bob Rowley. When we were children, none of us could catch you." Lowering her voice, she added, "But I don't think you'll be using that fine new plow you've won. How does your father's business prosper?"

"Your ladyship may tell Lady Louisa not to fret: The cham-peen will be here in good time for her party, and a cask o' brandy for the earl besides."

Honoria Capshaw, a beauty with flaxen curls and a classical profile, stood nearby, Tracy beside her. With a parting smile at young Mr. Rowley, Beryl went to speak to her future sister-in-law. Sidney had taken it upon himself to introduce Miss Selby to the vicar, and Lord Elston was crowded out by the gentlemen who surrounded Beryl.

Damon, reluctant to join any lady's court, kept his distance, although he watched Beryl from afar. "Who's that lad speaking to your sister?" he asked Louisa. "His face is familiar."

She looked away from her sons, who were proudly displaying their pet hedgehog to a cluster of village children. "It's Giles Capshaw, Honoria's brother. They don't resemble one another very much, do they? She is so fair, and he, poor lad, such a carrot-top."

"Their gorgon of a mother is little changed, I see," he commented. Louisa, smothering a laugh, told him to mind his tongue.

After all the other contests had concluded, the annual cricket match began, in which a team of

villagers battled a team boasting two of the earl's
sons as well as his servants. When a particularly
fine pitch drew faithful Giles Capshaw's attention
away from Beryl, she slipped out of the crowd,
bent upon escape, only to be intercepted by the
marquis.

"Are you so devoid of sisterly feeling that you
can desert Tracy and Cedric at such an anxious
time?" Damon quizzed her.

"I can't count the times I've watched them
play," she replied. "*Or* have had to hear Giles Capshaw crow about his prowess—which he never has
proved, being too careful of his clothes. I want to
visit the tinkers' stalls. Will you come?"

Damon agreed and went with her along a narrow footpath to the remnant of common grazing
land. "I enjoyed watching the face-pulling," he
told her when she asked his opinion of the various
competitions. "And the lady who wept when Louisa gave her the new coal scuttle. But I was even
more entertained when you presented the prize to
the ugliest man."

"Why? I do so every year."

"It was such a contrast, that poor fellow standing beside such a pretty girl."

Unruffled by his compliment, she said, "But
Rodney Judson isn't so very ugly. Not like Old
Bray, who had a most alarming face and always
won the pocket watch when I was a child. We
were quite fond of him, though, for he carved toys
out of wood—soldiers, and small boats, almost
anything." She looked over at Damon, her expression one of profound puzzlement. "Have you never
wondered why there's not a competition for the
*handsomest* man at a fair?"

"It must have something to do with masculine

vanity," he suggested. "With the present arrangement, we gain more by losing."

"I suppose so, for you gentlemen can be twice as vain as any lady! Consider Miss Capshaw—the most beautiful creature imaginable, and she cares nothing about her appearance. It's poor Giles who is so self-conscious, laboring over his neckcloth and the choice of a waistcoat, and he hates his red hair. I'm afraid he'd have no hope of being judged most comely."

"Whom do you consider to be the *nonpareil?*"

"You, of course, but your rank would prevent your being chosen," she mourned, picking her way carefully past some wild holly which threatened to tear her gown.

Accustomed though he was to admiration, her candid reply startled him. "I was correct in accusing you of disloyalty to your siblings. Do you not judge your brothers handsome?"

"Naturally, but how to choose from so many?" she said with a merry laugh, which made him wonder if she had been jesting all along.

They had reached the booths, and Beryl paused to look over the wares on display. One stall featured a selection of cheap and gaudy trinkets. "If you ask me very sweetly, perhaps I'll buy you a fairing," he told her, and when she seemed interested in a necklace of colored glass beads, he looked it over closely, searching for flaws in workmanship.

The tinker said proudly, " 'Tis Venetian work, smuggled goods, your worship. I've ne'er seen such a fine piece, and it will look well on your lady."

Beryl tugged at Damon's arm. "Let's move on," she urged him.

"Don't you like it?" he asked. "I think it quite pretty." He reached for his purse and counted out the full amount the man demanded. Later, as they made their way back to the village green, Beryl lectured him for handing over a sum she considered exorbitant, and only when he accused her of ingratitude did she cease to scold.

The cricket match was not declared until late in the afternoon, and afterwards there was dancing. Lord Rowan did not take part but his younger children did, with evident enjoyment. At first the nobly born, the gentry, and the common folk found partners among their own kind, but when Cedric deserted Beryl for a village maiden, his place was taken by Bob Rowley.

Damon, standing at the edge of the green, saw that the shaggy youth treated her with a rare combination of deference and familiarity, and was conscious of the same surge of jealousy he had known the day he'd met Dr. Shenstone. Through a cloud of dust raised by a dozen pairs of feet, he watched the slim, small figure dance down the set, but because Charlotte was near he had to maintain an expression of guarded nonchalance.

"What fun this has been," she commented when he escorted her to his curricle. "And how our friends would stare if they could see the dashing Miss Selby and the cool, supercilious marquis disporting themselves at a country fête. Frankly, Damon, I almost prefer this to those tedious, predictable evenings at Almack's, don't you?"

It was sundown by the time the Deerhurst party departed, the Kinnard men on horseback, Beryl and Louisa in the landau. Lord Rowan, leading the procession, turned his mind back to the days when his lady had presided over the festivities. An exultant Tracy was telling Cedric about his victory over the Capshaws, who had finally agreed that the engagement might be announced at the ball, but Cedric, wondering how to work a village dance into his nearly completed novel, made no comment. Sidney was also quiet, thinking how much he would like to return to the wars, but at least his temporary retirement had been enlivened by the presence of Miss Selby.

The two Kinnard ladies traveled in silence, until Beryl, hearing her sister's sigh, asked solicitously, "Are you weary?"

"A little," Louisa confessed. "Not surprising, considering that I spent the afternoon in conversation with Mrs. Capshaw. I thank heaven that of all our brothers it's Tracy who is marrying her precious daughter. He'll suffer no fools, and will deal admirably with his odious mother-in-law!"

"Does she still dislike the match now that he's a property owner?"

Louisa dismissed Mrs. Capshaw's objections with a disparaging wave of her hand. "Oh, no gentleman is a great enough match for Honoria, we all know that. But what angered me most of all was what she said about you."

"Me?"

"And Damon. She saw you coming out of the meadow together, and made a point of telling me all about his mistress, as though I were a green girl myself!"

"Oh, dear," murmured Beryl in sudden consternation. "I never thought it might be improper to take him to see the tinkers." She fingered her reticule, feeling for the bead necklace, wondering if she had made a mistake in accepting it. "Was it so very wrong?"

"Not at all," her sister declared emphatically. "Whatever reputation Damon enjoys amongst the Capshaws, he is first and foremost a gentleman. And it is nobody's business if he has mistresses. There's no Lady Elston to be bothered by it. He always conducts himself discreetly, although his liaisons always become known somehow. I daresay Eliza Preston has been giving herself airs, but she couldn't keep him to herself for very long. And you may be sure I gave Mrs. Capshaw a setdown, because I can't fathom how any of it concerns you."

"Nor I," Beryl said calmly. It didn't matter to her that Damon had cast off his mistress. But when she remembered his curious reaction the day she told him of Tracy's engagement, she asked, "Why is he so disdainful of marriage, do you think?"

Half-yawning, Louisa replied, "Because of his parents—his father, mostly. I'm sure he'd tell you about it, if only you asked."

"I couldn't," Beryl said quickly. "He'd think I was prying."

"Well," Louisa began, "it all began years ago, when Roger's Aunt Celesta Meriden went to Wiltshire to stay with her sister Alicia, the Viscountess Cavender. The Blythes had a neighbor, Beau Lovell—that's what he was called before he inherited his title. Beau courted the youngest Miss Meriden, and despite the fact that no one expected so proud a man to marry the daughter of an obscure Sussex baronet, he did just that. The marriage didn't prosper, though, and shortly after Damon was born, they separated. Lady Elston took her son to Elston Towers, and the marquis remained in London." Louisa paused and made an adjustment to her shawl.

"That is not so great a scandal," said a disappointed Beryl. "There are many such arrangements in high life."

"Wait till I'm done," Louisa admonished her. "The wits called them the Lovelesses, for Lord Elston's debauchery was widely known. But eventually a story began to circulate about her ladyship as well. Supposedly she had a lover living with her at the Towers. One summer she went to Bath to take the waters, and it was rumored that she had—well, that she was increasing. The marquis heard about it and set out from London, either to confront her or to comfort her, depending on whether you ask a Meriden or a Lovell." She paused, and continued in a near whisper, "When he got to Bath, Lady Elston was gone—she'd bolted with one of her grooms. Her husband overtook them, and to this day no one knows the fate of the groom or his relationship, if any, to Damon's mother. She and Lord Elston were on their way to the Towers when their carriage overturned."

Beryl was too shocked to comment.

"Damon was sent off to Eton and his fortune and property were administered by Roger's father, the sole trustee. The Lovells spent years trying to overset his guardianship, but to no avail, so Damon spent his school holidays here in Sussex. Later, of course, he learned to prefer London to the country. I believe he spends most of his time at balls and assemblies, and he has a box at *both* theaters, and the opera, too. Any woman who is seen there more than once is immediately accepted as his mistress."

"But has he never had a real sweetheart?" Beryl wondered.

"I heard that he almost offered for the Duke of Solway's niece. But Lady Miranda Peverel married Lord Cavender not long after he returned from Russia. Damon told me he helped to make the match himself, so he couldn't have been in love with her."

And he couldn't be so very prejudiced against matrimony, Beryl thought, if he had served as matchmaker for his cousin. Nor did she believe he was as aloof and unapproachable as he had once seemed, for he had mellowed considerably with each passing day. In his more outgoing moments, he was one of the most charming gentlemen she had ever known.

# 5

*And then mark what Damon tells his gentle maid,*
*And with his lesson register the deed.*
                              —RICHARD JAGO

The famed gardens of Deerhurst extended from
the rear of the house all the way to the glass-
paneled orangery. The landscape was formal, well
over a century old, and featured innumerable parterres which, like spokes of a wheel, converged at
a central fountain. All the walks were bordered
with flowering plants; roses abounded, planted in
formal beds, climbing the walls, and were trained
over an arched trellis to form a fragrant tunnel.
There was a Shakespeare garden and a large orchard, with groves of cherry, apple, pear, and
plum trees, and two labyrinths of shrubbery, one
in a circular pattern, the other a square. These
had been the haunts of generations of young Kinnards, who knew every twist and turn in the high
hedges where they often hid from each other, parents, or nurse.

The bowling green was also a favorite resort of
the young people, and one bright June afternoon
a lively group assembled there to watch Damon
and Roger, both coatless, play at battledore and
shuttlecock.

Beryl, seated on the grass, was oblivious to the contest as she read her second letter from Peter Yeates, disappointingly brief and devoid of loverlike effusions. He described his recent activities in a vague, haphazard fashion, and reiterated his desire to go to Brighton—not that she begrudged him a visit to the fashionable seaside resort. But she was disturbed by the tone of his missive, and tried to soothe herself with the reminder that gentlemen led very busy lives and were not always adept at expressing emotion. Even Tracy, now certain of the prize he had sought for so long, never alluded to his feelings for Honoria Capshaw, but no one doubted them.

After reading the note a second time, she tucked it into the pocket of her yellow gown and returned her attention to the game, only to find it was over. Damon, the victor, accepted the congratulations carelessly, swinging his long-handled battledore back and forth.

As the others began to gather their belongings and make for the house, he asked, "Who will join me for a stroll in the shrubbery?" Neither Charlotte nor Sidney was willing, Cedric had already vanished, and Tracy was escorting his betrothed to the house. Beryl was on the point of following them when Damon turned to her. "Won't you walk with me, Cousin Beryl?"

"If you wish," she answered readily, surprised and pleased by his invitation. He gratified her even more by admiring the grounds through which they strolled. "Grandfather Dirty Hands spent a fortune on the gardens," she told him, her eyes shining with pride. "He preserved our old-fashioned knot gardens and shrubbery walks at a time when every other gardener was digging them up."

"Why was he called Dirty Hands?"

"Like Papa, he was always digging about the place. We still have his silver-handled spade, which was given to me one birthday for my very own. He was quite a reactionary when it came to garden design, for when my grandmother wanted him to build a classical temple on that hill"—she indicated a small rise of ground beyond the orangery—"Grandfather Dirty Hands refused. He loathed the fashionable follies his friends erected on their lands, and quarreled with Lord Egremont when he took Capability Brown's advice and created an ornamental lake at Petworth House."

"But a Brown landscape is a prized possession," said Damon. "The park at Elston Towers is but a pale imitation, and unfortunately it hasn't been properly maintained. My land steward has suggested that I engage Humphrey Repton to undertake improvements."

Beryl turned a shocked face upon him, crying in dismay, "Pray do not mention that man's name in front of Papa, or he'll go up like a skyrocket! His loathing of all 'improving gentlemen' is as strong as his father's was! Do you know Sir Harry Fetherstonhaugh?" she asked with sudden intensity.

Damon deemed the question a *non sequitur*, but acknowledged the acquaintance, adding soberly, "He was a crony of my father's."

"When Sir Harry had a falling-out with the Prince of Wales—the Regent, I should say now—he retired to Uppark and consoled himself with additions to his house, with Mr. Repton advising him. Papa was appalled when his oldest friend paid 'that villain' fifty guineas for each visit. So please, no word of Repton if you value your neck!"

Damon halted before the entrance to the maze

and smiled down at her. "I promise, *petite*. As I never visit the Towers, the state of its park makes little difference to me."

They walked on, and Beryl drew in great breaths of damp and leaf-scented air. "How refreshing it is here!" she declared. "Have you learned your way to the center, where the benches are, or must I show you?"

"Surely you're not afraid to get lost with me?"

"Oh, no," she said, a trifle breathlessly.

They strolled on silently, Beryl discomposed by his question, and Damon no less so by her answer. She pulled a leaf from the hedge and folded it nervously, wondering if he was flirting with her. Always one to lessen strain whenever she encountered it, she inaugurated an unexceptionable topic of conversation—the weather—and the pleasant climatic conditions of Sussex occupied them until they reached the heart of the maze.

A trio of benches invited them to tarry, and Damon led her over to one of them. "Let us sit for a while, and you can share with me your impressions of the ancient city of York."

Gazing up at him in wonder, she asked, "Have *you* been there?"

"I seldom miss the August race meeting. You might not believe it, but I really am able to detach myself from London without any ill consequences. But we stray from the subject. How *did* you like York?"

"Very well. Aunt Sophia and I went to the Assembly Rooms every night, and to the theater. I covered every inch of the city wall and often attended service in the Minster."

"Will you mind living there, after you are wed?"

Reluctant to admit how little she knew about

her Peter's plans, she shrugged. "I can't say for
certain where Mr. Yeates will choose to live, for
we parted soon after pledging ourselves. As you
know, I haven't seen him since."

"He must have mentioned it in his letters,"
Damon persisted.

"His letters are . . . succinct," Beryl sighed. "I
do know that he is fixed in town for the remainder
of the Season, and expects to remove to Brighton
later."

"If he's so fond of society, I daresay you'll make
your home in London."

"Oh, I do hope not," she said involuntarily.
"That is, I prefer the country." After a pause she
ventured, "Doubtless you think my tastes insipid,
and perhaps Peter will too."

Damon repressed the urge to put a consoling
arm around her. He had begun to feel vaguely protective, as though he were in truth one of Beryl's
brothers, but at the same time there was something in his goodwill toward her that went beyond
mere friendly feeling. Certainly she was lovely and
spirited, though she was decidedly a hoyden, yet
at times she exhibited a quiet and impressive dig-
nity. She did not flaunt her woes, and only once
had her command over her feelings deserted her,
when she had learned of Tracy's engagement. And
she was loyal, for despite a long separation and
her father's vehement protest, she was still devoted to Yeates. As Damon had seen, she was a
graceful dancer and a horsewoman beyond com-
pare. None of these qualities in itself commanded
undue respect, but the combination was eminently
appealing.

She stood in need of a friend, he thought, for her
family seemed unable to support her adequately.

Sidney was too infirm, Cedric too curious, and Tracy too busy with his own affairs. Louisa's whole attention was on the forthcoming entertainments, however much she might long to see her sister settled, and as for Lord Rowan, Beryl could hardly seek solace from the one who was responsible for her predicament. And after sitting down beside her, he encouraged her to confide in him.

Beryl's sad story came tumbling out yet again, but it wasn't quite the same version she had told Sidney a fortnight ago. She found that in the interim she had forgotten a few details. For instance, she couldn't recall whether it was at their second meeting or their third that Mr. Yeates had escorted her to supper. Nor was she definite about when exactly he had first asked if he might call on her. Had it been a peach or was it cream—or both—to which he had likened her complexion? Not that she had any intention of repeating the compliment, but in the first days after her return from York, these pleasant memories had been her only comfort. Now, when she tried to describe Peter's appearance, she was certain only of the color of his hair, a tawny blond, altogether different from Damon's waving gilt locks. Her lover's complexion was bronze, whereas Damon's was alabaster white. Peter's eyes were dark and compelling. Looking into her companion's singularly beautiful eyes, she was reminded of the color of gentians or harebells.

Abruptly, without preamble or forethought, he asked, "Did he kiss you?"

"On the hand." She didn't blush or seem to be annoyed by the personal nature of his question, and Damon supposed the budding author's interrogations had left her impervious to prying. "We were in a public place when he proposed to me," she said sorrowfully, "and it's a great trial to me, not having been properly kissed by my betrothed." Damon grinned, and she said hastily, "Don't tease, I beg you!"

"I gather you've been properly kissed by someone. A local swain, perhaps?"

Beryl shook her head disconsolately, her long curls brushing against his coat. "The local swains, as you've seen, are a set of boys like Giles Capshaw, or ineligibles like Dr. Shenstone and Bob—" Suddenly mute, she blushed.

"What great shame are you concealing from me?"

"Something I had nearly forgot," she said with a laugh. "I *was* kissed once, although it was done quite improperly, I suspect. By Bob Rowley. He won the foot-race at the village fair and is one of the smuggling Rowleys, my father's tenants. Bob is exactly Ceddie's age and was very much about the place when we were growing up, and I often joined in their exploits. He kissed me once, in the Home Wood, a terrifying experience for both of us. Poor thing, he was afraid Papa would kill him for his presumption, and I knew Mama would scold, or send me back to school. No one ever found out, but from that day things changed between us, whether because of the kiss itself or the fact that we were growing apart, merely by growing older, I cannot say."

"And that was your only kiss, the clumsy salute of a tenant farmer's son? I suppose he gave you a quick peck on the cheek and that was it," Damon mused.

"Not at all! We kissed on the lips, and it wasn't

onesided, either, because I . . . well, I kissed him back."

"You shock me to the core."

"I was only fifteen," she said defensively.

He looked down at her, his eyes bright. "Seven years is a long time to be deprived of kisses. If you like, I'd be happy to remedy that, as well as demonstrate the correct technique. As a gesture of goodwill."

He placed his hands upon her shoulders, drawing her toward him so he could touch his mouth to hers, and although it was over in an instant, he continued to hold her, rather less gently than before.

After a moment of mutual scrutiny, he said lightly, "I'll beg your pardon, if you wish it."

"There's no need. I asked for it, more or less," she whispered. "But I don't want you to repeat the lesson, for my last kiss cost me a friend, and I like you too well to let a bit of foolishness in a shrubbery come between us."

Her reply stung and soothed him in equal measure, and he removed his hands from her shoulders. "I make friends by kissing, and without it would have none amongst your sex."

Beryl searched his face. "You've a great number of flirts, haven't you?"

"So it is said. You disapprove?"

His brittle smile was as much a weapon as his words, and Beryl looked toward the sundial, wishing she had the power to turn back time. Nothing was as it had been, and though his kiss had made her pulses race, she regretted it more than ever. Fiercely she said, "I had rather stay your friend than be your flirt, because I'm not cut out for both!"

Damon reached for one of her clenched hands and held it firmly, though she tried to pull it away. "What an odd child you are—and as such, quite safe from me. Now say you forgive me for thus sporting with you in the shade, and in return I vow never to do so again—unless you ask, of course."

"I do forgive you," she said, smiling again.

When she stood up and smoothed her gay yellow skirts, he could tell she had already put the episode behind her, but he could not. And he regretted that he was a man of honor, and she a nobleman's daughter.

For many years he had enjoyed his associations with ladies of high birth and easy virtue. Not all had courted his attentions, however, and if any female he pursued was too shy or unwilling to appreciate his gallantries, there were many others who did. Beryl Kinnard wasn't shy—far from it— nor had she demonstrated any unwillingness, not until afterward. It would be a joy to teach her more about her untried self and he fancied that he was as well qualified an instructor in the art of dalliance as could be found. She was a bud just beginning to unfold, and a few tender embraces might unfurl a new petal or two, but he was bound by a promise, the likes of which he had never made to any woman. And while he deplored it, he also applauded the discernment which had made her choose the golden value of friendship over the dross of less durable relationships.

A handsome traveling carriage with a crest emblazoned on the side panel had reached Deerhurst in their absence, and when Beryl and Damon returned to the house, they saw Jessom gloomily overseeing the unloading of baggage.

"The Blythes are here," Damon observed. "All four of them, judging from the number of trunks." Beryl paused on the steps, suddenly nervous about meeting a group of strangers, and he must have sensed her fears, because he tucked her arm in his and led her into the hall, saying, "They don't bite, *petite*. Dominic is my best friend. He and Justin are first cousins who wed cousins, for Nerissa and Mira are related to one another, though more distantly. I regard them all as family."

This assertion was proven by the affectionate greeting he bestowed upon the quartet. While Louisa was introducing Beryl to the newcomers, Damon shook hands with the handsome, black-haired Baron Blythe, then bowed over Lady Blythe's hand. He tossed off a friendly jest to Viscount Cavender, and kissed the cheek of the slender, lovely creature at his side.

"Admired Miranda," he said, gazing upon her fondly. "How fares my goddaughter, Juliet?"

"You should come to Wiltshire and see for yourself," she replied.

"We bring an abundance of family news," her husband added. He had a sensitive, fine-boned face and laughing brown eyes. "We spent the journey fighting over which of us would have the pleasure of telling it."

"It matters not," Louisa cried, "so long as someone tells us quickly! They've been tantalizing us with hints, so we know it concerns Mr. Meriden, the nabob."

"Surely our uncle hasn't cocked up his toes at last?" Damon asked. "Must we felicitate Justin on coming into that long-promised fortune?"

"Damon, really," Miranda said in reproof. "We don't wear mourning."

"It's not a death we've come to announce, but a marriage," Justin interjected. "Two days ago we attended a wedding at Bath Abbey. Uncle Isaac's wedding," he added, turning to Sir Roger Meriden.

The baronet looked perplexed. "Who on earth would he marry, at his age?"

"My mother," said Miranda quietly.

Beryl, standing forgotten in a corner, observed the various reactions. Louisa was astounded, as was her husband. With a happy laugh, Damon reached for Miranda's hand. "So, *chérie,* you and I are doubly related—first you wed my cousin, now my uncle becomes your stepfather. This is wonderful news indeed!"

Louisa shook her head. "But I don't understand. I thought Lady Swanborough was . . . ill."

"Not now, though it isn't widely known," Justin answered. "Neither is the fact that our uncle wanted to marry her years ago, when he was a wild young man. It wasn't till after his parents sent him off to India that she married Lord Swanborough."

Miranda raised her black head. "My mother's doctor in Bath has cured her. She's well enough to stay with us at Cavender Chase, and last year she was there at the same time Mr. Meriden was visiting."

Damon smiled. "Entirely by coincidence, or were you playing at matchmaker?"

"That's *your* game," Miranda said pointedly. "They met quite by accident. Mr. Meriden had never attempted to see her after he returned from India, though he knew she was a widow and was also living in Bath. He'd heard all the frightful stories about her mental decline and preferred to keep his happier memories intact. But when he saw her again, he was determined to remove her from Dr. Mostyn's house, where she has been living all these years. We were all pleasantly surprised when she actually accepted his offer of marriage, and she seems to be quite content with the new arrangement. He is very fond of her still, and loves pampering her."

"What a sweet story," Louisa said with a sentimental sigh.

"There will be an announcement in the newspapers sometime this week," Justin reported, "which will cause a great deal of comment. We thought it expedient to hide ourselves even deeper in the country, so here we are. My mother sends her warmest greetings to you, Roger. At present she's at Cavender Chase, looking after an army of little Blythes."

"And protecting Juliet from our Dickon, who is quite a bully," Nerissa Blythe added. "At least she has nothing to fear from Jamie yet; he's only two."

"Just the age I first began taking notice of females," commented Damon, and everyone laughed.

Lord Blythe told of their forthcoming journey to the Channel Islands, in his distinctive, husky voice. "When we leave Deerhurst, Nerissa and I will go to Portsmouth and board a vessel bound for St. Helier," he said. "Her mother was a Jerseywoman, and she has relatives there still. The children are old enough that we feel comfortable about leaving them for a few weeks."

Nerissa amended, "Not *completely* comfortable. But we leave them in capable hands, for Lady Cavender had two boys of her own and is the closest thing they have to a grandmother."

In Beryl's opinion, Lady Blythe was dismayingly beautiful. She had rich chestnut hair and full red lips, and was quite tall, though her husband was taller still. After Damon, Lord Blythe was the handsomest gentleman in the room, though Viscount Cavender was also quite attractive. Beryl didn't know what to think of Miranda, the lady once courted by Damon. She was more delicate than the dashing Nerissa, with darker hair and fairer skin, but both cousins had the same brilliantly blue eyes.

The arrival of the Blythes failed to overshadow what had occurred in the shrubbery, and for days afterward Beryl often speculated on how it might affect her relations with Lord Elston. His attitude toward her was changing, she was sure of it, and she hoped her behavior hadn't alienated him again.

If she could not completely forget his kiss, for great stretches of time she was able to think of other things. Fading memories of Peter Yeates were one refuge from thoughts of Damon, and with the concert drawing ever nearer, her music also consumed her. In her sleep she was haunted by the strains of the concerto, and as she took her daily exercise on her mare or worked her garden or strolled through the labyrinth alone, she hummed her harpsichord cadenza.

One day, when she intruded upon Cedric's unceasing literary labors, she discovered that he shared her preoccupation. As he frowned over his work, he whistled his flute solo. But the several sheets of foolscap spread out on his writing desk were blank, prompting Beryl to ask, "How does the great work proceed?"

With a sigh, he ran his perpetually ink-stained

fingers through his brown hair. "Nothing is coming along as I'd like. Though I'm very nearly finished, new ideas keep occurring all the time. I feel the way Herr Mann must do every time we take up our instruments: My characters are as stubborn as we are in failing to please!"

She said sympathetically, "It must be a hardship, setting aside your work so often for rehearsals."

"Oh, I don't mind so much; sometimes it's a relief." He directed a penetrating glance at his sister and asked suddenly, "I say, Beryl, what news of Mr. Yeates? Didn't you receive a letter?"

Regarding the toes of her black kid slippers, she replied, "Nearly a week ago. He keeps terribly busy. It's a very social place, London."

"Oh, I expect so," Cedric agreed.

She knew he hadn't been taken in by her pretense of unconcern. If he hadn't inquired into her thoughts and feelings, they must be all too apparent. With a sigh, she said, "You should have taken Tracy's romance as the model for your book. I *am* glad for him," she added quickly, "for I'm sure during his years in the Peninsula he believed his case with Honoria to be hopeless. Anyway," she concluded on a cheerier note, "good things are said to come three at a time. We've had Louisa's happy news about her new baby, now there's Tracy's engagement. Surely I shall be the next to win my heart's desire."

Cedric said he hoped it would be so, biting back a reminder that it was ill fortune which came by threes, not good.

# 6

*He loves to sit and hear me sing*
*Then laughing, sports and plays with me.*
— WILLIAM BLAKE

Sir Roger Meriden shared Damon's fondness for racing, and maintained a small but flourishing stud at Fairdown. Desirous of improving his stock, he enjoined his cousins and Lord Blythe to assist him, and one day they set out hopefully for Goodwood, only to return at midday, bemoaning their ill luck. The viscount and the baron went off to find their wives, leaving it to Roger and Damon to describe their fruitless journey.

They found Louisa in the library, her sewing basket beside her, watching her sons play with a set of lead soldiers. Beryl had joined in the game, and she and Jack were pelting Sidney with questions about military tactics. Cedric, seated at his writing desk, penned a letter to Miss Jane Austen, and paid little attention to his brother-in-law's discourse.

"Why don't you try Sir Harry Fetherstonhaugh's stables?" Beryl asked. "He must keep a dozen or more thoroughbreds at Uppark."

Sidney looked up from the *Sussex Weekly Advertiser.* "She's right, Roger."

"So she is," the baronet conceded, "and Sir Harry will likely be glad to have the purchase money for his rebuilding schemes. Beryl, my poppet, I owe you a favor—what is your desire?"

"Take me to Uppark," she answered promptly.

Louisa, quick to protest, said gravely, "Even if Roger consented, I could never allow you to go. Uppark is a bachelor establishment, and if you went there with a party of gentlemen it would be scandalous!"

Roger, who deferred to his spouse in all matters of propriety, did not argue.

Although Sir Harry Fetherstonhaugh was of respectable birth and a long established friend of the family, he had once been a crony of the Prince Regent's. Lord Rowan sometimes invited him to Deerhurst, but when Beryl pointed this out, Louisa shook her head and declared that their parent would never permit his unmarried daughter to visit Uppark without sufficient chaperonage. Sir Harry was a rake of the first order, and now that his mother was dead he had no lady to receive for him. There might be a female in residence, Louisa said darkly, but of the sort who would do a young lady's reputation more harm than good.

Beryl said wistfully, "But I do so want to see the house, and the horses."

Master Jack Meriden, who had just bowled down a line regiment of toy soldiers with an orange, added his piping voice to the fray. "Take me to see the horses! Mama, please say Harry and I may go, too!"

"Now look what you've done," moaned Louisa.

But Beryl had not yet given up the heaven-sent opportunity to view the splendors of Sir Harry's estate. Going to sit by her sister, she said in her

most coaxing manner, "Dearest Louisa, won't you
go with me as my chaperone? You've been moped
here at Deerhurst for so long, entertaining half the
world and his wife. A day's outing will do you
good. Won't it be pleasant for her, Roger?"

Smiling at his wife, the baronet said, "To be
sure, my love, it will put roses in your cheeks.
Beryl would not let it be otherwise."

Everyone laughed, even Louisa. Beryl, sensing
that she was close to victory, continued, "You can
make the journey in Damon's curricle, and he'll
take care to drive ever so slowly so you won't feel
the bumps in the road. Won't you?" she demanded
of the marquis, who nodded. "Surely you won't
refuse; you aren't so stuffy as that."

This was a master stroke, for Louisa prided herself on her broad-mindedness, and there was nothing she disliked so much as being thought a prude.
But she would not capitulate too easily. "I expect
you mean to gallop across country like a hoyden,
in that deplorable gray habit."

"I promise to wear the blue one and ride very
sedately, dearest sister."

"You are a troublesome, spoiled girl, and I'm
mad as a March hare to consent. I have no interest
in racehorses or riding about in curricles in my
condition, but I daresay our guests would enjoy
the excursion." Louisa gathered together her sewing and her sons, and with a long-suffering glance
at the triumphant Beryl, she left the room, followed by her husband.

When Damon bore Sidney off for a game of billiards, only Cedric remained with Beryl. He'd finished his letter and had stretched out on the sofa,
his eyes closed. The completed manuscript lay
abandoned on his writing table, temptingly within

reach. Beryl carried it over to the window seat, and for the rest of the afternoon the only sounds in the room were the ticking of the long-case clock in the corner, Cedric's snores, and the rapid turning of pages.

The novel traced a difficult love affair much like Beryl's. Lady Frances, the heroine, met her Mr. Thompkins during a visit to a distant town, and returned home to apprise her father of her desire to wed. He refused his consent, citing a long-standing feud between the two families, of which the hopeful lovers had been entirely unaware. Cedric's detailed description of a country summer included some familiar elements—a nobleman's visit, a village fair—and in the course of the narrative he satirized several local persons, most notably the toplofty Mrs. Capshaw and jovial Sir Harry Fetherstonhaugh. But truth and fiction diverged in places. The lovers managed to meet secretly several times, assisted by Lord Llewellyn, who acted as go-between and was secretly in love with Lady Frances. Beryl deduced that Damon had been the model for the noble baron.

The romantic passages were affecting but never cloyed by sentiment; the tone throughout was one of gentle irony and boundless humor. The heroine was depicted in a more human fashion than was common, and the only character with whom Beryl found any fault was Thompkins, the idealistic young hero. To her mind Lord Llewellyn—handsome, unselfish, and so heartbreakingly attached to the lady—was the more admirable of the two men. And when she reached the final, decisive chapter, she was conscious of a vague disappointment, although it contained the happy outcome which figured in her own nightly prayers.

The persistent chime of the clock striking five woke Cedric, and when he saw that his novel was strewn across the window seat, he smiled sleepily at his sister. "How much have you read?"

"All of it," she confessed.

He sat up, suddenly alert. "Well? What did you think?"

"You are wondrous talented, Ceddie, and I liked it very much."

"I had the greatest difficulty with the ending, and I'm not convinced I've got it right yet." Hunching his thin shoulders, he added, "I might've let Llewellyn marry Lady Frances. He'd prefer it that way, I'm sure."

Beryl, who hoped the union of the heroine and her hero foretold a similar future for herself and Peter Yeates, might have opposed him, but she remained silent.

"But," he went on, "I'm leaving the book, as it stands, until I learn Miss Jane's opinion. As a published author, she will know what, if anything, might improve the book. I've decided to call it *The Clandestine Betrothal.*"

After endorsing this choice, she listened to his tentative plans for his second book, which, to her great relief, had nothing to do with separated lovers.

The most scenic approach to Uppark was a steep and winding carriageway shaded by beeches and chestnut trees and Scots firs. Beryl and Roger, on horseback, were the first of the Deerhurst party to arrive at the imposing Golden Gates at the entrance to the park; Damon's curricle and the landau bearing Lord and Lady Blythe made the ascent of the hillside more slowly. The brick house was the same age as Deerhurst, and had been similar in design before the addition of the new entrance on the north front, a Doric portico of Portland stone connected to the main building by a corridor.

After handing Louisa out of the curricle, Damon said to Beryl, "So, my lady, what do you think of Mr. Repton's skills?"

"I preferred the house as it was." Then she added candidly, "Although I scarcely remember what it was like," which made her tormenter laugh.

A footman took them to the ivory and gold saloon, its high ceiling decorated with delicate plasterwork in the Adam style. At either end of the room hung portraits of King George and Queen Charlotte in their coronation robes, and the French brocade curtains were drawn up to admit the sunlight. Florid Sir Harry greeted his guests warmly, and was particularly attentive to the ladies. "Lady Louisa, and little Lady Beryl, too," he said gaily, after welcoming the Blythes. "It's not often I have the pleasure of entertaining so many charming creatures all at once. Repton's portico is a work of art, eh?"

Conscious of Damon's merciless eyes boring into her, Beryl joined the others in expressing admiration.

"So, Roger, you want to look over my horses. Excellent, excellent. I'll parade them before you as the Grand Turk does his harem, I will."

Beryl had to bite her lip when she observed her sister's horrified reception of an analogy unsuitable for virgin ears. Sir Harry, oblivious to Louisa's distress, continued, "Ladies, please to make yourselves comfortable, my house and servants are at your command. The housekeeper will be glad to conduct your ladyships through the principal rooms while we fellows visit the stable block. I've ordered a cold collation to be laid out in the dining room in half an hour.''

To Louisa's obvious relief, the housekeeper turned out to be a woman of respectable mien and years. She was also knowledgeable about the elegant furnishings, many of which had been purchased by Sir Harry's parents during a lengthy Continental tour. Taking the guests upstairs to the chamber preferred by the Prince Regent, she showed them a damaged leg on one of the Chinese lacquer cabinets and explained that one of the royal dogs had been tethered to it.

When Beryl criticized this mode of confinement, the housekeeper pointed out the dark stains on the damask bedcurtains, saying, "I'm afraid the animal did far more harm when he was permitted to roam, my lady.''

"I should think the Prince would make sure his dogs are housebroken,'' Beryl laughed. "Our Gypsy would never so forget herself!''

Her favorite object in a dwelling crammed with beauties was the doll's house which had belonged to the late Lady Fetherstonhaugh. Seven feet high, it had nine rooms, all inhabited by ladies and gentlemen and servants in their proper attire. Completely appointed in miniature, it was furnished with fourposter beds and chairs, and tables laid out with silver candlesticks and cutlery, and even a set of Waterford glassware.

The housekeeper left the ladies in the red drawing room, after directing their attention to the portrait of Sir Harry as a young man, which had been painted in Rome. The windows were open, and the air pleasantly scented with the mignonette and heliotrope blooming outside.

"Charlotte and the Cavenders missed a great treat by staying at home. I think I never saw a house so perfect," Beryl commented. "It might be a royal residence."

"It very nearly was," said her sister. "When Sir Harry and the Prince were on terms, His Royal Highness was forever driving over to Uppark from Brighton for parties and races. Mama and Papa sometimes attended musical evenings here in those days, but they would never bring me."

A little while later the entire party sat down to a light meal in the gold and white dining room, still in the process of being restyled by Mr. Repton. Their host pointed out the decorative plaster busts of such famous personalities as Napoleon, Charles James Fox, and Sir Harry's good friend the Duke of Bedford, and he commended his architect's many talents so often that Beryl had to cover her quivering mouth with her napkin. He also took great pleasure in recounting hunt meetings and racing parties of bygone days. "Ah, yes," he said, smiling reminiscently, "this room has heard much in the way of laughter and witty conversation. Have I ever told you about my dancing girl, Lady Beryl?"

She shook her head.

"She was near sixteen when I brought her to Uppark—as a servant, you understand, for at that time my mother was in charge of the household. A clever little lass, my Emma, and many men envied me: Greville, Willet-Payne, and anyone else who met her. Well do I remember the night when she entertained us by dancing on this very tabletop for a select party of gentlemen. The Duke of

Queensbury was here, and Lord Grosvenor, and I
believe your father was also one of the company,
Elston. He had an eye for a pretty lass." Sir Harry
paused to sip his wine, unaware of Damon's scowl
and Louisa's smoldering eyes.

"What was I saying? Oh, yes, Emma Hart. Eventually I had to send her away, which was tiresome,
but how could I acknowledge the bast—that is,
my mother couldn't know about—well, it became
necessary for her to leave Uppark," he concluded
with a belated attempt at discretion. After a self-
conscious cough, he went on, "Later she was
painted by a great man, Romney, and married
very well for a Cheshire blacksmith's daughter.
Can you guess the identity of my little Emma,
Lady Beryl? No? But she married Sir William
Hamilton, our ambassador to the court of Naples,
and had Lord Nelson for her lover—the greatest
hero of our age."

"It was Lady Hamilton who danced upon your
table?" Like most young women of her generation,
Beryl had a general knowledge of the scandal
which had resulted from the Hamiltons' close
friendship with Britain's naval hero.

"She's quite fat now," Sir Harry sighed. "Poor
Emma, she hasn't a groat to her name, despite
Admiral Nelson's good intentions toward her and
the little Horatia. I've lent her money when she
needed it, and often send gifts of game in the
shooting season, in memory of the lively times we
had together here at Uppark."

This blithe comment goaded Louisa past bearing, and she kicked her spouse under the table.
Roger, after exchanging a glance with his out-
raged wife, promptly stated his desire to try the
paces of a particular horse.

" 'Twas Jupiter who caught your eye, eh?" Sir Harry asked. "He's out of Don Josef's line—the horse I rode to victory myself back in 'eighty-four, beating Sir John Lade on the Prince's Hermit. We raced on West Harting Down, and I won fifty guineas." Rising, he said, "Lady Louisa, Lady Blythe, I urge you to inspect the gardens, for they're looking very fine just now. I suspect Lady Beryl, being a horsewoman, will want to go with us."

Damon cornered Louisa and said firmly, "You and Nerissa do as he suggests. I'll take care of your sister."

"Oh, very well, but promise me you'll keep her away from the stables—and that old court card. If Papa knew Sir Harry had entertained Beryl with stories of his horrid Emma, we'd never hear the end of it!" She shook her head, and Damon laughed.

A few minutes later, Beryl asked what had so amused him, but he refused to tell her. "You think my sister is being silly," she hazarded. "So do I, especially since she's the one who informed me about the existence of females of—of that sort."

"Spare my blushes, I beg you."

"Did *you* know Sir Harry was Lady Hamilton's first protector?"

"Yes, but I confess my father's acquaintance with the notorious Emma comes as a surprise." Like Louisa, he wished the old man had kept his unsavory recollections to himself. "From all I've ever heard of my parent, his escapades at Uppark were probably the most creditable of his career."

"You always frown when you speak of him."

"Then I'll be careful not to do so," he said lightly. "And you, my dear, are always smiling."

"I most certainly am not!" Beryl protested. "Not *always.*"

"It seems so to me, but perhaps it's just the way your mouth turns up at the corners," he said as they entered the saloon. "And now we find ourselves alone together for the first time since our pleasant discussion in the labyrinth." When she averted her face, he teased, "Are you afraid Sir Harry's tales may have a corrupting influence on me? Perhaps it's the air of Uppark, scented as it is with scandal."

"If you're trying to alarm me, you won't succeed." Making her way to the pianoforte, she sat upon the silk-covered bench and ran her fingers lightly over the keyboard. "I'll play for you, if you wish. Have you a favorite song?"

"I'm rather fond of the one you played my first night at Deerhurst. ' 'Twas in the pleasant month of May, in the springtime of the year . . .' "

" 'The Merry Haymakers,' " she said brightly. "I like it too. Will you sing with me?"

But Damon remembered only the first verse, so the duet soon became a solo. Leaning against the instrument, he gazed down at the fair singer, whose clear, true soprano was ideally suited to the simple song.

When Beryl was done, she wrinkled her brow in thought. "Do you know 'The Laboring Man's Daughter'?"

"Every word," he answered proudly. "I'll sing the nobleman's part and you can take that of his sweetheart."

She began to play, and together they sang the opening stanzas. Then Damon sang alone:

"I never have seen you but once in my life,
  And then in the dream you lay by me
  But now I'm beside you, by the look in your eyes,
  I know that you ne'er will deny me."

Beryl, her cheeks pink, continued:

"O what's your desire, pray tell me kind sir
  That you're so afraid of denial?
  Although I am poor, no scorn I'll endure,
  Do not put me under any such trial."

When his arm closed around her waist, she lifted
her hands from the keys and said accusingly, "You
are a shocking creature—and I was a fool to be so
taken in!"

"Your singing has bewitched me, *petite*."

He leaned closer, but she drew back. "Damon,
someone might come in."

"You neither swoon nor slap me," he whispered,
his lips close to her ear, "as a proper young lady
should." But he released her, knowing he could do
nothing else. However provocative she was in her
close-fitting riding dress, she was absurdly innocent—and she was also, to his regret, pledged to
another man. And it would be cruelly unfair to
toy with her when he could offer nothing in return
but fleeting physical pleasure and a lasting shame.

When Sir Harry and the other gentlemen returned to the house, they invited Damon to join
them in the little parlor, where the two baronets
haggled over a mutually agreeable price for Jupiter. As soon as they emerged, the sale concluded,
Sir Harry insisted on showing his guests the view
from the south lawn. They dutifully admired the

herd of deer cropping the turf while their host pointed out the Isle of Wight in the distance.

"Mr. Repton says that any alteration or addition to the existing landscape would be superfluous," he reported.

"That is a point in Repton's favor, you must admit," Damon murmured to Beryl. "At least his genius prompted him to leave nature alone."

"As Papa's daughter and a true descendant of Grandfather Dirty Hands, I cannot agree that he *is* a genius," she retorted.

When the carriages and horses were brought forward, Sir Harry drew Damon aside. "Forgive me if I made you uncomfortable by mentioning your father. For all he was a hard man, and died in damned strange fashion, he was a lively fellow once . . . ah, well, we all were in those days. I flatter myself that I was his closest friend."

"He hadn't many," Damon said coolly.

"Nor have I, not any longer. The Argylls, the Bedfords—they look in on me from time to time, but I'm more often alone than not. But happy in that," he added hastily. "And whenever I hear about the exploits of Brummell and the Regent and that set, I don't regret living here in retirement, amusing myself as I please and subject to the whims of no man but myself."

But his brave speech failed to convince Damon, who had perceived the underlying bitterness. He guessed that Sir Harry missed playing the part of court jester, and still pined for those who had all but forgotten his existence.

"That one has grown into a pretty lass," the baronet said, eyeing Beryl. "Thinking of slipping your neck into the noose, eh?"

"You are mistaken, sir," Damon told him frostily.

He could hardly admit that his designs on Lady Beryl's lovely person were entirely dishonorable.

"Ah, well, I can understand your reluctance. I've been a bachelor nigh on threescore years!" the older man declared, puffing out his chest.

As his curricle followed the riders and the landau along the winding drive, Damon wondered if he would end his days in the same solitary fashion as Sir Harry. How would he feel, thirty years hence, living alone, a gentleman of taste and wealth and wide experience, with no serious occupation apart from embellishing the house his ancestors had built? It seemed a dismal prospect to an active, virile young man, mad with desire for a charming young woman and with no hope of ever possessing her.

# 7

*Damon is practis'd in the modish life.*
— JOHN GAY

With each passing day, Damon became more fascinated with Lord Rowan's daughter, and more concerned that Charlotte, an exceedingly observant female, was aware of it. To prevent his one-sided flirtation from finding its way into the gossip which circulated from drawing room to dinner table to bedchamber, he resolved to keep his distance in future. And while his decision was born from a sense of self-preservation, he also felt he had a duty to protect Beryl, who did not deserve to be made notorious.

So he avoided her. He spent his days riding with Roger, or fishing the local streams with Sidney and Tracy, and whenever he walked in the gardens, he did so with the Blythes and the Cavenders. In the evening he partnered his host at the card table and sat up late with the other gentlemen, drinking and talking. All in all, he was well entertained, yet he was not entirely at ease. He was even less so on those rare occasions he did encounter Beryl, usually when the musicians met to rehearse.

On the day of the concert he rose uncharacteristically early, and despite his valet's protests that none but servants should stir at that hour, went down to the dining room. He regretted it when he found Beryl there, having just returned from a long ramble with Gypsy. "You've been out already?" he asked, taking his usual place across from hers.

"Yes, and met Bob Rowley in the Home Wood."

"An assignation with your former flirt?" he quizzed her. "You'll make me jealous."

"It wasn't an assignation, we came upon one another entirely by chance. Poor Bob was up all night, unloading cargo. He left a cask of brandy in the hay-barn, but we must send a cart to fetch the champagne from the Rowleys' hiding place, there's so much. It will have to be smuggled into the cellars so Tracy won't find out!"

She was entirely lovely this morning, her face slightly flushed and her eyes bright with excitement. Her morning walk had left her disheveled: her brown curls were mussed, and the ribbon holding them back was off-center.

"Please don't tell Louisa I was in the woods alone," Beryl begged him. "I'm afraid she wouldn't approve. Papa and I used to walk or ride there every morning, but not since—not since I returned from York." She leaned her elbows on the table, resting her chin on her upturned palms. "Are you nervous about the concert?"

"Not so much as I probably should be," he confessed. "And you?"

"Oh, yes," she replied unabashedly. "I'm worried that all the notes will fly right out of my head as soon as I sit down to play! It would be a pity to disgrace Herr Mann, after he has taken such pains with us." She added, "But I'm even more terrified of meeting the Wainworths and your friend Mr. Hughes."

"Why?" he asked, looking up from spreading raspberry preserves on a slice of toast.

"They'll think I'm dowdy and countrified. *And* gauche. Don't you?"

"Of course not." Although he had indeed been highly critical of her at first, time had revised his opinion. Many of those qualities he'd regarded as defects in her now delighted him.

"Whenever Miss Selby walks into the room," she sighed, "I feel like a bumpkin."

"Charlotte's well enough in her way, but hardly a beauty."

"Lady Blythe and Lady Cavender are beautiful."

"I won't deny it. But greatly though I admire them, I am not unconscious of the attraction of wood nymphs, especially ones with eyes like jewels. What's the matter, don't you like compliments?"

"Not yours. And I hate flirting!" She pulled a face.

Beryl spent the rest of the morning chasing down various servants and conveying Louisa's orders, and by the time the last of the company arrived she was weary and flustered and even more concerned about making a bad impression. Lord and Lady Wainworth were fashionable newlyweds, London friends of Damon's, as were the lady and gentleman who came with them. Lady Wainworth and Lady Martha Onslow greeted Miss Selby with an extravagant show of affection, but as Beryl took them upstairs, they laughed unkindly behind their hands and made harsh comments about how hagged poor Charlotte seemed.

That night the butterflies wheeling and tumbling in Beryl's stomach kept her from doing justice to the excellent dinner, and she ate only a little of the buttered lobster and other dishes her sister had judged suitable for such high company. Seated as she was between Sir Harry Fetherston-haugh and Tracy, she was not required to exert herself, and was therefore able to observe the rest of the company through discreetly lowered lashes. It was sufficient to nod her head in the baronet's direction every so often as he held forth on his expectations of the next race meeting at Good-wood, and her brother was conversing with Lady Cavender, who looked like an angel in ivory satin. Louisa was very handsome in a gown some two seasons old, new to the outsiders if not to the neighbors, her eyes shining with triumph as she gazed upon her assembled guests. Charlotte Selby chatted with the elegant Mr. Davenant Hughes in her animated style, occasionally bestowing a friendly smile upon Giles Capshaw, seated on her other side. She was draped in saffron-colored silk, cut low to display a ruby pendant which glittered on her pale breast like a spot of blood. The magnificent toilettes on display caused Beryl to despise her choice of white muslin ornamented with green ribbons. And though she was wearing the glass beads Damon had given her, he hadn't noticed; throughout dinner he flirted with the languid Lady Wainworth, who pointedly ignored her bridegroom.

When Jessom laid out the port and brandy decanters on the sideboard, the ladies retired to the drawing room to discuss persons and events utterly alien to Beryl. She sat quietly in a corner, praying that her fellow musicians wouldn't partake too liberally of the post-dinner libations. And when the gentlemen emerged, she was relieved to see that none of her relatives, nor the marquis, exhibited the flush commonly brought on by excess.

She waited for Damon to approach her—surely he must know she stood in need of his lighthearted reassurances—but he allowed himself to be accosted by Lady Wainworth. Within a few minutes he moved on to the buxom, apple-cheeked Lady Martha Onslow. By the time he joined Lady Cavender on the settee, Beryl was grateful for the attentions of Giles Capshaw. His blind adoration might be a joke to her family, but tonight she excused his preoccupation with his appearance, and readily forgave him for not being tall or blond, or a handsome marquis.

Damon, taking the vacant place beside Miranda, asked, "Are you enjoying yourself here at Deerhurst?"

"Very much," she told him. "I welcomed this opportunity to know Justin's *other* cousin. I quite like Sir Roger and Lady Louisa and their sons."

Her wistful reference to the Meriden boys did not go unnoticed. Placing his hand over hers, Damon said, "Mira, Mira, don't go borrowing trouble."

"I'm not. But Juliet will turn two at the end of the year, and I had hoped to—to present her with a playmate by now."

"Nerissa went even longer before she provided her Dickon with a little brother. And I believe your brother Ninian made an appearance at least a decade after you did."

"I know. Justin keeps reminding me of that," she said with a smile. "Did he tell you we're going to London when we leave Deerhurst? He says he must support Canning if the Catholic question is raised in Parliament, but he also means to consult with his lawyer. Certain arrangements would have to be made to ensure that our daughter would inherit Cavender Chase in default of heirs male. Otherwise the estate, like the title, would pass directly to Dominic."

"Justin is simply being his usual careful self. His brother Ramsey died unexpectedly, so naturally he wants to keep his own affairs in order." Seeing that this worried her more than it comforted her, Damon added, "I doubt that he despairs of having a son to succeed him. Blythes generally produce nothing but. There hadn't been a daughter in the family for generations, till Juliet was born."

Miranda turned her deep blue eyes from her husband, who stood across the room, back to Damon. "And when are you coming to visit her? You needn't go near Elston Towers if you don't care to; we'll be happy to keep you at the Chase."

"You are kind, but I dare not accept. It's all too apparent that Dominic has infected Justin with an enthusiasm for farming, and I'm impervious to the charms of sheep and cows and hens."

She did not press him, and merely shook her head at his stubborn aversion to his native shire.

A few minutes later Louisa invited the company into the music room, and as the members of the orchestra took their places, the laughter and chatter ceased. The ladies fanned themselves gently while the gentlemen settled back in the gilt chairs, anticipating a half-hour of boredom before they could return to their flirtations and discussions of horses and harvests.

Herr Mann made a brief speech, explaining that Bach had composed the concerto in D nearly a hundred years ago, one of several pieces dedicated to the Margrave Christian Ludwig of Brandenburg. Then he took up his violin, cast an anxious smile upon his players, and nodded.

The bows moved in unison, bringing forth bright notes from violins, violas, and cello, and Cedric's fingers danced along his silver flute. Beryl's hands flew across the keyboard, and Sidney tapped his foot in time, turning her pages with brisk efficiency. The sprightly first *Allegro*, the longest movement, featured a harpsichord cadenza lasting a full sixty-five measures, with innumerable trills requiring swift accuracy. Beryl performed this difficult solo with aplomb, and a hum of appreciation went up from the audience, only to be drowned out as the other instruments joined in.

The musicians eased into the slower, haunting *Affetuoso*, dominated by the flute and the strings. Although the harpsichord part was less flashy, the appreciative eyes of Mr. Davenant Hughes and Lord Wainworth remained fixed on the slim figure in white surrounded by a sea of dark coats. The second *Allegro* was light and gay, punctuated by shimmering notes from the harpsichord and the lilting strains of the flute. When the orchestra arrived at the finale, their efforts were rewarded with applause from many pairs of gloved hands.

Beryl, thankful to be finished, sat quite still, her heart thudding and her head light. As her confederates bowed, instruments in hand, she rose from the bench to curtsy. Damon caught her eye and smiled—the first time he had deigned to notice her—and she inclined her head in polite but distant acknowledgement. He'd made clear his preference for more exalted company than hers now that it was available to him, and his shallowness pained her.

Miss Shenstone, a garrulous spinster of some forty years, approached her to say, "Your performance was faultless, Lady Beryl, simply faultless. My brother has told me so often of your skill on the harpsichord, although to be sure, I've heard you play the pianoforte many times. And who would guess the earl could sit still long enough to play a concerto? Such a busy, active gentleman, and always on his horse." The doctor shook his head repressively, as if fearful that his sister's ready tongue might give offense.

In their determined effort to commend Beryl's performance, Lord Wainworth and Mr. Hughes crowded out Giles Capshaw. His lordship led her out of the crush and procured a glass of champagne from a passing footman, while Mr. Hughes begged to know if Herr Mann was available to instruct his sisters. Unaccustomed to exciting such intense interest, Beryl accepted the drink with a murmur of thanks, and nodded at Mr. Hughes, who looked as if his whole life depended upon a good report of the music master's abilities. As her cavaliers exerted themselves to charm her and the champagne took effect, she began to feel more at ease and less conscious of what Damon was doing. And only after her father led the gentlemen away to the library for a game of whist did she remember that she should have asked if they had ever met Mr. Yeates in London.

Cedric, who stood nearby talking with Damon and Lady Wainworth, called to her to come and settle a dispute. "Now, Beryl," he said, "please tell them Papa spent as much money on the new pigsties as he did on his hunters last year, for they won't believe me."

After offering the confirmation he sought, Beryl

explained, "Our father is exceedingly fond of his pigs. He visits them every day." She couldn't resist adding, "And I'm sure he'd be delighted to show them to your ladyship."

"My dear Elston," Lady Wainworth trilled, raising her eyebrows at Damon, "you have certainly entrenched yourself in the country with a vengeance. And has the earl given you a spade and set you to work in the gardens?"

"No, Geraldine, he has not."

"I'm relieved to hear it. I trust you aren't going to rusticate forever. Or have the pleasures of country life, whatever they may be, superseded those of society?"

Damon removed an enamelled snuffbox from his coat pocket and when he had taken a delicate pinch, he answered, "Oh, no, the garden of London will forever be my favorite. There are so many fair flowers to be found there."

Beryl, stunned by his perfidy in aligning himself with a mocking, spiteful female, had to escape or else disgrace herself by making an offensive retort. Her brother followed, pulling her aside in time to prevent a collision with a footman and his tray. "Odious woman," she spat as he guided her out of the way. "She was insulting our family, and our home. Damon, too—I shall never forgive him!"

"He was only jesting," Cedric said soothingly. "That's just their way. It's not fashionable to admit to liking things over-much." Beryl gave a disbelieving toss of her head before exiting through the tall, glass-paned door leading onto the terrace. She hoped a few breaths of fresh air would soothe her raging temper.

Damon, watching her leave the room, longed to go with her, but Lady Wainworth forestalled him by saying in lofty condemnation, "Whatever her talents at the keyboard, that chit wants better manners—and dressing. I really wonder at Louisa Meriden. She should have removed her sister from this den of masculinity years ago. All those brothers, to say nothing of the earl! A gentleman like that ought not to have sole charge of a daughter, it never answers, and I suspect Lady Beryl is one of those hard-riding females as a result." Heedless of Damon's threatening frown, she continued, "She'll suffer for it, you mark my words. Marriages are made in ballrooms, not on the hunting field, and someone had better give her a hint."

Charlotte Selby passed by, her gloved hand on Captain Kinnard's good arm, and paused to ask, "What can you be saying, Geraldine, to make my cousin glower so?"

Lady Wainworth, unable to repeat her remarks in front of Lady Beryl's brother, said quickly, "Nothing of importance, my dear. Do excuse me, Elston, for I must discover if my spouse has yet managed to game away my dowry."

When the lady hurried away, Charlotte gave a curt, derisive laugh. "If I were Geraldine, I'd refrain from making remarks that might lend credence to all the worst rumors about me. The tattlemongers say Wainworth would never have married our sharp-tongued friend if not for her handsome portion."

"She's not the only one who can cut with words!" Damon retorted. "Sheathe your claws, Charlotte, you've shocked Sidney."

Lady Wainworth's acid commentary had incensed him, but he set it down to spite: her hard-won husband had very nearly made a fool of himself over the younger girl. His own behavior was nothing to boast of, however. He had gallantly dallied with those ladies who expected it of him, but his heart hadn't been in it. Desperate for Beryl's more forthright discourse, he stepped out onto the terrace, and when she turned toward him, a stream of reproach flowed from her eyes.

"Your playing was magnificent," Damon told her.

"Your lordship is too kind," she murmured with what he considered an excess of sarcasm.

"Not kind, only truthful. You've had a great success, *petite*."

"I may have been acclaimed by the gentlemen, but their ladies are not disposed to be polite." She added scathingly, "Not that I care for their opinion."

"Geraldine was jealous."

"Why should she be jealous of me? They are a breed apart, these fine friends of yours, with their silks and jewels and airs, and I am lost in all that dazzle."

"Ah, no," he said softly, "for the white butterfly stands out among those more garishly tinted, and always will."

"Your compliments are too practiced and insincere, Lord Elston. Go spill them into the ears of Lady Wainworth, or Lady Martha—or Lady Cavender." His show of concern kindled her resentment; she would not be patronized.

"With you I do not dissemble." He reached out to touch her necklace, and when his fingers closed around the glass beads they grazed her skin. "This becomes you well, as I knew it would."

She couldn't let him know how his proximity unsettled her, or that he had disappointed her. He was entirely different tonight from the Damon she was beginning to know. Now he was once more that radiant, remote being she had worshipped from afar so many years ago, a creature from a distant world. She knew he would one day return to the whirl of gaiety that was London, and their fragile friendship would be a thing forgotten in the hectic activity of balls, routs, and promenades. There was no reason why any of this should matter to her, for in all likelihood she would forget him just as quickly.

Damon saw the tears on her lashes, sparkling like tiny diamonds in the light of the flambeaux, and knew he was perilously close to making the sort of declaration he would regret. "Sweet Beryl, do not cry. I never meant what I said to Geraldine."

"It isn't that," she asserted stiffly.

"No?" He moved even closer.

"I miss Peter."

Damon stared down at her, too stunned to make a reply. All the time he'd believed her to be suffering from his neglect, she had been mourning the absence of her lover instead, and it was a blow to his pride.

At that moment Cedric stepped outside, a brimming glass of champagne in one hand. "Here's something for you, Beryl," her brother announced cheerfully. "I had the devil's own time getting it, though, for Louisa declares none of the family can have any more, or there won't be enough for the ball."

"You didn't have to take the trouble of bringing it. I was about to go myself," she said, taking the glass. As Cedric accompanied her indoors, he glanced uncertainly over his shoulder.

Damon, alone in the flickering torchlight, was furious with Beryl for summoning the specter of

Peter Yeates, and even angrier at himself for dropping his careful pretense of disinterest. In that dangerous moment of certainty, now thankfully past, he might have said anything, done anything, and would certainly have paid a price. He ought to be glad there was a Mr. Yeates, he thought savagely, and then he tried to convince himself, not for the first time, that this was only a passing fancy that couldn't outlast the summer.

When he rejoined the revelers in the brightly lit music room, the elegant ladies greeted him happily. Said Lady Martha Onslow, "You stood out there such a long time, my lord, and looked so fierce I feared you might smash one of the window-panes! Shall we go in to supper now?"

Damon escorted her to the dining room, where cold meats and cheese and other delicacies had been set out. But to his surprise and dismay, he discovered that all desire for food and flirtation had deserted him.

# 8

*Her gesture, motion, and her smiles*
*Her wit, her voice, my heart beguiles.*
                                    —Anonymous

"You're an early riser today," Lord Rowan commented when his daughter entered the dining room.

Beryl, her face a study of weariness and trouble, gave him a wan smile. She had been awake for many hours, haunted by the memory of the lie she'd told Damon last night. Not entirely a lie, she consoled herself, because she had missed Peter—although not until after Damon had snubbed her.

"Come and see the new piglets," her father invited her when she had finished her breakfast of tea and fresh buns.

Eager to set her troubles aside for a space, she accepted, and together they walked to the small farm which supplied Deerhurst with meat and poultry, milk and grain. Several neat brick structures enclosed a central yard, and the new pigsties had been erected beside the dairy, in order that his lordship's beloved animals might be near the whey and buttermilk on which they fed. One of his many innovations was a water cistern in which his pigs could be washed, and there was a separate yard for the hogs being fattened, with its own trough and straw-ricks.

The earl gently poked each of the new piglets with his walking stick, then moved on to inspect a prize breeding sow, her mouth full of straw as she carried it to a corner of her pen to make a nest. These frantic preparations pleased his lordship, who nodded in satisfaction. He and Beryl crossed the yard, where chickens knelt down in the dust to clean themselves, to look over the henhouse. After a brief discussion with the poultrywoman, he proposed a walk through the gardens.

"Our musical evening was quite a success," he said in tone of self-congratulation. " 'Tis my belief we pleased the company with our playing."

"Yes, Papa," replied a subdued Beryl.

"And I saw how those young fellows mobbed you afterwards," he continued. "Louisa's been telling me these three years that you should've been presented to society, but to my mind it makes no difference. Everyone recognizes a true gentlewoman, whether or not she has curtsied to the Queen or toadied to those stiff-necked patronesses at Almack's!"

Deeming it wiser to agree with him rather than dispute his simplistic view, she murmured assent. He was so blinded by affection that he would never realize the limitations imposed by her upbringing. It wasn't true, she had discovered, that town people and country folk were essentially the same; during a long, sleepless night she had forever discarded that erroneous belief.

Warming to his theme, Lord Rowan went on, "Now, Damon Lovell has never been above his company, for all his blood is as blue as it comes and his pedigree one of the longest in England. I've nothing against Lord Cavender; his mother was a Meriden, after all. And Baron Blythe is a fine fellow, and quite knowledgeable about farming. Their wives are pleasant young women, and Miss Selby is a well-bred creature, anyone can see that. But those Wainworths, and that fellow Hughes!" He shook his head in disgust. "As vulgar a lot as I've ever met, whatever their titles and wealth. They might have come out of a counting house. Such a disappointment the younger generation is—oh, never you, puss, or your brothers and sisters, even if Emily is as toplofty as she can stare and Tom so ordinary."

Beryl squeezed his arm fondly. It had been many weeks since they'd had one of their talks, not since she had returned from York.

"So much has changed in my lifetime," Lord Rowan said thoughtfully. "Men of my day studied the classics, we made the Grand Tour as a necessary part of our education, frolicked or settled down to marriage as we willed, and thought to raise up our children in our own image, as our fathers did before us. Some of us failed—even poor Farmer George, whose German queen bore him a litter of nincompoops. The Duke of York's mistress, that Clarke woman, led him by the nose and right into a scandal; his brother the Regent has two wives, and cleaves to neither!"

"Oh, Papa," said Beryl, smiling up at him, "your arguments are as old as man and as current as the letters in the *Times*, condemning modern-day morals."

This walk, like so many in the past, ended in the shade of the Earl's Grove. It contained five ornamental trees—the rowan, the oak, the willow, an aspen, and *Nyssa sylvatica*—and was so called because the combination of their first letters spelled out the family title.

"How d'you intend to spend this day of our great ball?" the earl asked when they turned back to the house.

"Seeing to the entertainment of our guests. Possibly we can have a game of lawn bowls later, or make an excursion to Goodwood, or Petworth."

Lord Rowan opined that the weather would be too oppressive for an afternoon drive. Gazing up at the sky in his knowledgeable fashion, he added that there was every likelihood of a thunderstorm later. "Can't I tempt you to ride to Chichester with me?"

"I wish I might, but I mustn't abandon Louisa, when she arranged this party for my amusement. Tomorrow, perhaps?"

"Tracy and I are off to London in the morning," he reminded her. "That firebrand Canning is determined to raise the Catholic question again, and likely there will be a motion. I want to cast my own vote rather than rely on a proxy."

"Oh, I do wish these troublesome people had never come!" Beryl cried. But her discontent was a product of something besides the impossibility of riding with her father. She blamed their company for the perplexing alteration in Damon's behavior toward her.

Miss Charlotte Selby, the first houseguest to show herself downstairs, entered the library shortly after noon and found Beryl there, inspecting a book of fashion plates. "You've chosen a fine retreat," she said approvingly. "It promises to be a warm day, and this room has the welcome aspect of a cool cave." Beryl nodded, and for several seconds they stared at one another wordlessly. It was Charlotte, the more socially adept of the pair, who found herself at a loss, for she was taken aback by the considering expression in her ladyship's green eyes.

"Miss Selby, I wish to beg a favor," Beryl said suddenly.

"Do call me Charlotte, please. My cousin is known as Damon in this house, so there can be no excuse for formality between us. How may I help you?"

"By assisting me with my toilette for the ball. I—I wish to make a more creditable appearance than I did last night."

Charlotte smiled and replied, "My dear Beryl, you may have felt less than adequate in your white muslin, but we in our silks and gauzes envied you your complexion, your beauty, and your admirers. As for lending you my aid—I warn you, I never tamper with perfection." But Beryl's forlorn face made her revise her decision, and she amended, "Oh, very well, if you are so set on it, I shall send my maid to dress your hair and will select your jewelry myself."

Beryl held out her book. "I was thinking this style of coiffure might be an improvement." As Charlotte glanced at the engraving, she added, "You may wonder at my request, but there is a—a certain gentleman, and—"

"Yes, I know," Charlotte interrupted her, "and I assure you nothing could please me more. The instant I laid eyes on you, I picked you out for Damon."

The color flew from the younger girl's cheeks. Shaking her head, she said breathlessly, "You are mistaken. I cannot conceive why you should think that he—that I—oh, *no!*" She paused to collect herself, then continued, "I was referring to Mr. Yeates. He has been living very high since we parted, and I don't want to disappoint him by my lack of polish when we meet again."

Charlotte gazed back at Beryl, her eyes narrowed. "Is your suitor so exacting?"

Beryl hesitated, for Damon had entered the library, handsomely dressed in a blue coat and biscuit-colored pantaloons, looking rather cross. He claimed to have no appetite, despite missing breakfast, but did not protest when Beryl rang for tea and cakes. While she and his cousin continued to examine the fashion journal, he nibbled at the food, then hid his face behind a newspaper.

"Here's a set of persons bent on improving themselves!" Lord Rowan commented when he barged in upon them an hour later.

Beryl climbed to her feet. "Returned already, Papa?" Beaming down at her, he fished a tiny leather box from his coat pocket. "What's this?" she wondered when he handed it to her.

"It looks suspiciously and most deliciously like a jewel case," observed Charlotte. "Open it, my dear. I'm in a fever of curiosity."

Obediently she lifted the lid to disclose a pair of tearshaped pearls lying on a nest of crimson velvet. "Oh, Papa," she breathed, "how lovely."

Pleased by her admiration of his gift, and by Charlotte's envious sigh, Lord Rowan said, "I thought you needed cheering up, puss. It's naught but a trifle, but Louisa was saying the other day that you should have some ear-drops to wear with your mother's necklet."

After giving him a grateful kiss on the cheek, she

tucked her arm in his, saying, "Let's show them to her. And you must praise her for what she's done to the saloon—it has been transformed into a ballroom since you saw it last."

When the father and daughter withdrew, Charlotte declared wonderingly, "Never before have I known a gentleman to dote so upon a female child! It's a wonder she hasn't been thoroughly spoilt by it."

"I fancy growing up with eight siblings is in part responsible for her amazing lack of self-interest," said Damon, affecting boredom.

"I daresay, but they seem to dote on her as much as Lord Rowan does. Well, I repeat what I said when I first came to Deerhurst: you are to be congratulated. She really is charming, and her family are your dearest friends—so comfortable for you both."

"Sweet coz, you seem to forget Mr. Yeates," he said, turning his attention back to the newspaper.

"No, for we were discussing him before you came into the room. I'm convinced he's hopelessly ineligible, and if it's any comfort to you, she's barely acquainted with him."

"Foolish Charlie, I stand in no need of comfort."

Charlotte plucked the newspaper from his hands, commanding his whole attention. With a wicked smile, she asked, "Did you expect to marry your first love? Of course not; no one does. A first love is a necessary evil, and must be got over like—like the measles, or a first toss on the hunting field. Don't laugh! I tell you Lady Beryl's attachment to Mr. Yeates is in a very precarious state." She reached out to ruffle the golden helmet of his hair, too perfectly and precisely groomed to suit her eccentric tastes.

"That may be, but it's hardly my concern."

His stubborn insistence that he cared nothing kindled Charlotte's wrath but she knew better than to plague him.

She kept her promise to supervise Beryl's preparations for the ball, and when they presented themselves in the drawing room, the admiring glances Beryl received were a fitting tribute to her beauty, Charlotte's taste, and the French maidservant's skill. Beryl's long brown curls were dressed high, giving her a more mature look, as did her mother's pearl necklace and the matching eardrops her father had provided. The ballgown of pale green gauze over a cream silk petticoat, never before worn, was simple but elegant. What pleased Charlotte most of all was that although her protégée's looks were enhanced and improved by her attire and the new style of hairdressing, she was clearly recognizable as herself. Watching her, Charlotte acknowledged the truth of something she'd read in one of the many tomes on proper deportment pressed upon her by her mother, that a woman is never so beautiful as when she does not know it.

The dinner preceding the ball was even more magnificent than that of the previous night. Thirty people partook of beef *à la' royal*, *soupe* Lorraine, Florentine rabbits, salmon, prawns, aspics, a variety of vegetables in season, cakes, and hothouse fruit.

As the summer sky finally began to darken, the other guests arrived. The saloon, lit by chandeliers and sconces, had not looked so fine for many years. The yellow brocade curtains, recently taken down and thoroughly cleaned, shone like new. Louisa had also seen to it that the gilded frame of every mirror and painting was carefully dusted with a piece of cotton wool.

Hired musicians from Chichester took up their instruments, and Lord Elston, the nobleman of highest rank, opened the dancing with the daughter of the house.

He wore a black coat and white breeches, and his hair gleamed like gold in the candlelight. As they came together in the stately allemande, he murmured, "Is your ladyship in the mood for compliments?"

Beryl's gaze veered downward. "That depends," she answered, "on the nature of the compliment." She had decided to play his game tonight, and if he was in a mood to flirt, then flirt she would. If he ignored her, he could expect similar treatment.

They were separated by the figure of the dance, then met again. "However many partners I have this evening," Damon continued, his voice low and caressing, "not a one of them will be as fair as my first."

At this, her first grand ball, Beryl was not the wallflower she'd feared she might be. She danced every set before the supper break, when her father signaled for silence so he and Mr. Capshaw could make a formal announcement of Honoria's engagement to Tracy. Numerous toasts followed, and the neighborhood folk, knowing of the couple's long attachment, were especially pleased. The dowagers seated on the sidelines and at the card tables began speculating on the probable size of Miss Capshaw's dowry, and the nature of Tracy's expectations as heir to his godfather in Kent.

Beryl's pleasure was slightly marred when Damon chose Lady Wainworth as his supper partner, and she accepted the escort of the exquisitely

dressed Mr. Hughes with an overbright smile.
When he set about entertaining her with anec-
dotes about society people, she feigned interest
and avoided the temptation to let her gaze wander
in Damon's direction.

When the gentleman paused for a sip of the
smuggled champagne, she said, "Mr. Hughes, I
wonder if you have ever met Mr. Peter Yeates in
London?"

Without even considering, he replied carelessly,
"Shouldn't think so," and embarked upon a con-
voluted tale about his friend Lord Petersham and
a tea-merchant.

Lady Wainworth, observing this tête-à-tête from
across the room, turned to Lady Martha Onslow.
"I expected Davenant Hughes to invite you to sup
with him, my dear, but that country maiden has
been flirting with him so furiously he never had a
chance."

Lady Martha, covetous of Mr. Hughes's name
and long rent roll, tittered self-consciously, and
her round cheeks were unbecomingly flushed.

"You may safely leave it to me to detach him
from Lady Beryl," Damon said coolly.

When Beryl saw him bearing down upon her,
she hid her pleasure beneath an attitude of studied
disinterest, a trick she had learned from him. After
a brief exchange with Mr. Hughes, he bore her
away, leading her past the crush in the saloon and
through the tall doors. Beryl offered no protest
when she found herself on the terrace, although
she remembered only too well how uncomfortable
a place she had found it the night before.

As he led her out of the torchlight, she asked,
"Why have you stolen me away from Mr. Hughes?

Not that I'm not grateful, for his stories were frightfully dull!"

"Is that why you were laughing at them?"

Her eyes flashed at the implied criticism. "Unfair, when you've made your preference for giddiness in ladies abundantly plain!" she cried.

"That being true," he said smoothly, reaching for her hand, "I have spirited you away for a bit of moonlight dalliance. Do you object?"

"There is no moon tonight," Beryl murmured inconsequentially. "The clouds are moving in from the sea, and the stars are hazy—we'll have rain later."

"If you expect to divert me by talking of the weather, as though I were Davenant Hughes, you're wasting your breath. I require rather more of you, sweet Beryl. Can you guess what it may be?" He heard her soft gasp and saw the accompanying rise and full of her breasts, partly revealed by the cut of her bodice. Leaning closer, he inhaled her lavender scent, then said, "One kiss only, that is all I desire." He took her in his arms, thankful for the darkness which concealed them, and when she lifted her face to his, he covered her lips with his own. "You learn very quickly," he whispered hoarsely. "Still, you might improve with further instruction. Happily, I am here to provide it." But before he could suit the action to the word, he heard footsteps coming along one of the garden paths. Stepping away from Beryl, he gestured at the skies with one arm and said in a carrying voice, "Yes, indeed, I do believe there is a shooting star, just to the left of that cloud."

Beryl, struggling to reassemble her scattered wits, turned and saw a lady and gentleman coming around the side of the house, hand in hand.

From the sweetly bemused faces of the engaged couple, she surmised that Tracy and Honoria had been busy with some star-gazing of their own.

The first flash and crash of a violent thunderstorm interrupted Beryl's dreams in the early hours of the morning, but eventually the sound and fury gave way to a gentle shower and she was coaxed back into sleep by the soothing wash of rain against her bedroom window.

The change in the weather delayed the break-up of the party and the guests, less than eager to spend the day plowing along the muddy roads to Brighton or Portsmouth, remained at Deerhurst. Lord Rowan, after consulting with Tracy, decided to delay his own departure for London. The subsequent discovery that his library had become a gentlemen's lounge put him in a foul temper, and he stalked off to the estate office, settling down with a well-thumbed copy of *The Compleat Angler*. A few minutes later he was dozing peacefully in his chair.

The drawing room was taken over by the ladies, their hands occupied with needlework while they discussed the ball. Beryl, unable to support this tortuous inactivity, made her escape as soon as she dared. Roger had braved the rain and brought his sons over from Fairdown for the day, so she invited Jack and Harry to join her in fashioning an armada of paper boats to float in the brook. This enterprise was shortly abandoned for the livelier game of their own devising, "Hunting for Harry." After granting the younger boy a generous quarter of an hour to secret himself somewhere in the house, Beryl and Jack set out in hot pursuit. Their search came to an abrupt halt when the latter burst into the estate office, shouting that he was on the scent, and received a scold from his irate grandpapa. Eventually he and his aunt gave up and went to the kitchens to coax some gooseberry tarts from the cook.

Harry was not seen until the afternoon, when a startled housemaid discovered him in one of the linen closets, sound asleep.

The bad weather persisted for two days more. On the morning the sun chose to reappear, Lord Rowan and Tracy departed for London after an early breakfast. The second carriage to drive away was the one bearing the Blythe clan to Portsmouth, where Dominic and Nerissa would board the ship bound for Jersey.

As they proceeded along the muddy highway, Miranda felt queasy. She tried to tell herself the constant swaying of the vehicle was responsible, yet she couldn't suppress the hope that this might be the first sign of the longed-for second child. As a consequence, she contributed very little to the ensuing discussion of the past week.

"I enjoyed myself thoroughly," Nerissa declared in her hearty way. "Deerhurst is as lovely as its reputation led me to expect, and the Kinnards are so friendly and unpretentious. It was an interesting mix of people, don't you agree?"

Her husband nodded but maintained that some of the guests had seemed out of place. "What could our hostess have been thinking, to invite that stick Davenant Hughes, and the Wainworths?"

"She asked them on Damon's account. I believe he is very thick with them," Nerissa answered. "But he, too, was rather out of place. Curious that he should choose to spend his summer in Sussex, when he refuses to set foot in Wiltshire."

Justin opened his eyes to say, "He spent part of his youth here—the happier part."

"Well, I wouldn't have teased him for the world, but it's obvious he has a new flirt in Lady Beryl Kinnard," said Nerissa. "I wonder if anything will come of it this time?"

Miranda said mildly, "Damon will never marry."

"You think not? Well, I suppose you know best," Nerissa sighed before turning to the window to study the scenery.

The Wainworths' carriage was the last one to set out from Deerhurst. They had expected Lord Elston to go with them, and his polite refusal had vastly disappointed the ladies. Just why he chose to remain buried in the country was the subject of an exhaustive debate between Lady Wainworth and Lady Martha Onslow during their drive to Brighton, but neither of them touched on the truth.

# 9

*Our Chawton home, how much we find*
*Already in it, to our mind;*
*And how convinced, that when complete*
*It will all other houses beat.*

—JANE AUSTEN

In the absence of the earl, his children managed to keep busy about the house and the estate, and the continued improvement in the weather permitted any number of outdoor pursuits in which they were joined by their two remaining guests. Sidney spent his days on horseback, supervising the haycutters; Cedric was working diligently to make a clean copy of his manuscript for Miss Austen's perusal and seldom strayed from the house. Damon passed a great deal of time with his cousin Roger as they debated a legal matter, and he even sent for his London attorney to attend their discussions. A document was drawn up, and on the day it was signed, Roger and Louisa emerged from the library wearing grave expressions, but none of the parties involved would reveal exactly what had occurred behind the closed door.

Beryl took advantage of the warm days to putter about in her lavender beds, her hands encased in protective leather gauntlets, while Gypsy, the spaniel, lolled in a patch of sunshine. And while she plucked weeds and worked the soil with her silver-handled spade, she generally thought about Damon.

His voice, his touch, his warm smiles all had an unsettling effect upon her. For many weeks she had responded to his persistent gallantries with mingled amusement and dismay, but ever since he'd held her in his arms on the torchlit terrace, her emotions had been in turmoil. Her guilty pleasure in another man's company forced her to examine her readiness to be married to Peter, and when many days went by with no word from Brighton, she saw it as a reproach for her faithlessness.

She did receive one letter that week, which contributed to her unease, posted from London and written in her father's flourishing hand. When the groom who regularly brought the post from the receiving office in Chichester delivered it to her, she abandoned a lively game of lawn bowls to read the single sheet addressed to "Dearest Puss." It contained a wealth of fatherly affection, a modicum of political news, and closed with an inquiry about the welfare of the earl's pigs.

With a sigh, Beryl refolded the note, reflecting that her life, once a simple, settled thing, was filled with uncertainty and conflicting desires. Formerly she had aspired to be a dutiful daughter, worthy of her papa's love and respect, until her yearning for Peter Yeates had divided her loyalties. What a sorry pass her stubborn folly had brought her to, she thought despondently, for how could she cut herself off from him, possibly forever, and live out her days in the cold north—or in London—with a young man she barely knew?

It was obvious to her now, as never before, that all of her present sorrows had resulted from the hasty pledge she had made in York. As she considered her predicament, she recognized her desire to be more than a friend to Damon, that her fondness for him was in truth something else entirely. And if, as it seemed, he was also fond of her, he could do nothing about it while she was engaged to someone else. If she had fallen in love with the marquis, it was imperative that she apprise Peter of the change in her sentiments as soon as possible. To cry off by letter was impossible. His direction was unknown to her, nor was she certain that he was still in Brighton. But somehow she had to free herself from an entanglement which had become undesirable.

Her decision made, she felt as if she had successfully forded a deep, wide river. Behind her was the familiar, comfortable landscape of the past, and now she stood in alien territory.

A few minutes later, when Damon came walking toward her, she experienced trepidation, exhilaration, but, strongest of all, hope. And with his approach her pulses began to flutter in the most absurd fashion—only one of several symptoms which had plagued her since the night of the ball.

"It will soon be your turn to bowl again," he told her. Glancing down at the crumpled paper in her hand, his lip curled. "Has Mr. Yeates written again?"

With tolerable composure she answered, "No, not for several weeks. My letter comes from Papa."

"No bad news from London, I trust."

"No news at all, except that he misses Deerhurst."

"And you."

"Well," she replied, "he did mention his pigs,

too. I daresay they are more worthy of his affection, considering how wicked and willful I've been of late."

Damon laughed at her woebegone expression. "There's not a wicked bone in your body. I'd have discovered it long ere this, villain that I am." His voice softened, and his eyes were mild and kind, even a little sad, when he said, "I hope you know that if I can help you in any way, you have only to ask." This was perhaps the most unselfish offer he had ever made, and it was a costly one. But at that moment, if he had possessed the power to conjure up Mr. Yeates and deliver him to Beryl, he would have done so just to make her smile.

"Thank you, but I know what I must do now." She rose from the garden seat, still clutching her letter, as though she intended to carry out her resolve at once. "I came close to making a serious mistake. I nearly ruined my life, as dramatic as it sounds."

Damon suspected, from her talk of wickedness and ruining her life, that she had contemplated some drastic action, most likely an elopement to the Border, and his relief that she had reconsidered was overpowering. By the time they returned to the bowling green, she was as merry and carefree as he had ever seen her, laughing back at Cedric when he challenged her to improve upon his last shot. It was as though her despondency had lifted from her shoulders only to descend upon his, Damon thought morosely when she bent down to take her aim.

The bowl's drunken, uneven tumble ended only a few inches short of the white jack, and Beryl clapped her hands, crying triumphantly, "There now, Ceddie, can you do better than that?"

Watching her caper about the lawn, Damon reminded himself that he had known of her romance from the day he'd met her. Yet for some reason he had never accepted her marriage as anything more than a remote possibility, when in fact it was inevitable. As his affection for her had increased, so had his desire, and had she been someone other than her own sweet self, he might have the comfort of knowing that he could woo her to his bed after her marriage, as he had so many dissatisfied society matrons. But Beryl was too fine, too rare a being to play her husband false, and where she loved, she loved completely. She would be irrevocably lost to him when she wed her precious Peter Yeates, but how, he wondered, could she be any more lost to him than she was now?

He had always been more or less comfortable with the solitary path he had chosen, yet as his eyes followed her, he envied the unknown, untitled gentleman who rejoiced in the name of Yeates.

Not only did Miss Jane Austen write to say she would receive Cedric; the day fixed for the journey into Hampshire dawned fair and mercifully dry. In the morning a pair of vehicles left Deerhurst, Damon's curricle, in which Cedric traveled, and the landau carrying his sister and Damon's cousin. Beryl wore a summery cotton frock with alternating stripes of coral and white, and her broadbrimmed *bergère* hat of straw was decorated with ribbons and artificial blossoms. Her companion was striking in a smart pelisse of lilac-colored cloth and a white gown.

In the course of their journey they passed hills and dales, wood and meadow, and many a field where the last of the hay was being gathered. They stopped for refreshment at Petersfield before joining the Gosport road, which carried them north toward the town of Alton. The gentlemen in the lighter, swifter curricle were the first to reach the tiny hamlet of Faringdon, and Cedric, who had been reading the signposts carefully, advised the marquis to slow his pace, as they were but a mile from Chawton.

Pointing to a manor house on their right, he said excitedly, "That will be Mr. Edward Austen's house. Pull over, Damon, and let's wait for the landau to catch up. We're nearly there."

The cottage they sought was situated at the intersection of the Winchester and Gosport turnpikes. A square house of red brick with a tiled roof and sash windows, it sat across the road from a horse-pond, and what appeared to be a spacious garden was enclosed by a tall wooden fence and a hornbeam hedge. Several beech trees and firs also provided much-needed privacy to a residence inconveniently bordered by highway on two sides.

As soon as the carriage bearing the ladies arrived, Damon handed over his reins to one of the grooms, while Cedric, his precious manuscript clutched to his chest, walked up to the front door and beat a brief tattoo with the knocker.

A startled housemaid ushered the foursome into a small drawing room and left them there. Within a few minutes a handsome woman with sharply aquiline features and dark hair partly covered by an elaborate cap entered, and after a quizzical glance at the company, she asked which gentleman was Mr. Kinnard.

Cedric, gazing at her with rapt attention, replied, "I am. Thank you so much for giving me permission to come, Miss Austen. Here is my novel," he said, presenting the stack of pages.

The lady did not take it from him, but said, "I'm the wrong Miss Austen—poor Betsy was so muddled that she came to me rather than going to Jane. She's across the hall, likely working so hard she failed to hear the knocker. Pray excuse me, and I shall fetch her for you." After she left the room, the visitors could hear the opening of a door followed by the murmur of feminine voices.

Miss Austen soon returned with another lady, who greatly resembled her. Miss Jane was younger than her sister, but she was also tall and had dark, curling hair tucked under a ribbon-trimmed cap. A plain white gown accentuated the bright color of her full cheeks, and she had a quick, light step. If she was startled by the number of strangers in the drawing room, she managed to hide it, and smiled when she shook hands with her fervent admirer.

As she chatted amiably with the ladies and gentlemen, the author surveyed them with her sharp hazel eyes, drawing rapid impressions from all she observed. The vivacious Miss Selby was too dashing and worldly to suit her quieter tastes, but Jane had a weakness for fashion and therefore admired the lady's style of dressing. And despite her tendency to be critical of young ladies, she detected no fault in Lady Beryl Kinnard, who possessed a pleasing combination of rational conversation, graceful manners, and a lovely face. And judging from Mr. Kinnard's frank enthusiasm, he was just as charming and unaffected as his sister. Jane was much struck by Lord Elston's appearance and address, and though she was half inclined to dismiss it as an old-maidish fancy, she rather supposed he was the suitor of the lady in the striped gown.

"It must seem odd," Lady Beryl said to her, "that so many of us should have come with Ceddie, but his lordship and Charlotte and I were too much intrigued to stay at home."

"Is the chance of meeting an obscure lady novelist such a temptation?" asked Jane, with a humorous twist to her small mouth. "My brother Henry is the most delightful of men, present company excepted, but his pride in my success sometimes exceeds my own. I have often taken him to task for telling people of his connection to the unknown author of *Sense and Sensibility*. And though I hope my second book sells, I most definitely do not intend to let myself become a wild beast on display."

Cassandra Austen nodded sympathetically at her sister. "We've been at great pains to keep the secret of Jane's occupation from our Chawton neighbors—indeed, from most of our relations as well!"

Fixing the unassuming authoress with her black gaze, Charlotte Selby asked, "And what is to be the title of your next work, ma'am?"

"It was originally called *First Impressions*, but in the process of lopping and cropping, I've decided upon another: *Pride and Pejudice*. That insipid phrase 'by a Lady' will, I trust, be changed to 'by the author of *Sense and Sensibility*.' "

Beryl, looking out of the gothic-styled window, commented on the charming prospect of trees and flowers, and the elder sister smiled. "I would expect one of your family to incline toward gardens, Lady Beryl. We've always heard of the beauties of Deerhurst, being somewhat addicted to gardening ourselves—my mother most particularly. One of her summer colds prevents her from receiving you today, but our great friend Miss Lloyd, who is sitting with her, should be down soon."

Jane, suspecting that the youth at her side was impatient with the small talk, climbed to her feet. "Mr. Kinnard requested an interview, so I must beg you to excuse us for a time. Bring your manuscript, sir, and we can review it together in the sitting-room. I will apologize for its sad state. I've been working there all morning."

As Cedric was led away, Cassandra Austen said, "I would be most happy to show you Chawton Park Wood, if you're not too fatigued by your journey. There are some very fine beeches, and it's one of our favorite walks."

This plan being agreeable, they set out at once. Upon learning that Mr. Edward Austen also possessed a property in Kent, Beryl monopolized their guide, asking her any question about the county where Tracy and Honoria would make their home.

"I admit to being favorably impressed by the lady novelist," Damon told Charlotte as they trailed behind Beryl and Miss Austen.

"Well, the elder sister is the handsomer of the two," she maintained, "though I cannot criticize any spinster, being one myself. At first glance, Miss Jane seems too retiring to have written so interesting a novel as hers is, yet she has visited London, and the family lived in Bath for a time. I expect they are both uncommonly clever. I wonder they do not grow bored with this rural existence."

"Have you found the country so very dull, Charlie?" Damon quizzed her.

"I'm a town creature, you know it well—and I believed you to be the same." After giving him one of her sly looks, she paused to pluck a wild rose from the hedgerow. "Shall you retire to Elston Towers after your marriage, leaving the London ladies bereft of your so delightful company?"

"My dear coz, this new inquisitiveness does not become you. I warn you, if you don't soon recover from the malady, I'll have to take steps to effect a speedy cure." Damon brandished his ebony walking-stick in a menacing fashion.

"I will be good," she promised, fluttering her lashes in pretended alarm. "Do not beat me, I beg you, or worse, send me back to Mama—not yet. I've got quite a nice little flirtation going with Captain Kinnard, and not even you could be so cold-hearted as to banish me from Deerhurst before I weary of it."

As Miss Austen had said, the magnificent beeches were the chief beauty of Chawton Park Wood. At the end of the pleasant ramble, Beryl asked if they might also see the Great House and the village church, but Charlotte, less hardy than she, pleaded weary feet.

"If Miss Austen will point out the way I'll go with you," said Damon. Her grateful smile was like a ray of sunshine, and he felt amply rewarded—not that it was in any way a sacrifice, for he welcomed the opportunity to be alone with her.

After they inspected the dark and silent church of St. Nicholas and had strolled the grounds of Mr. Austen's Elizabethan mansion, Beryl expressed her readiness to return to the cottage. "I quite like Miss Jane," she told Damon as they walked along a lane overhung with trees. "At first I thought she was shy, for although she seemed gratified by our praise, she was reluctant to discuss her work. And it's a pity she so dislikes the notion of becoming famous. If I had written a novel as fine as hers, I'd want everybody to know!"

"Shall we determine her skill as a gardener before we rejoin the others?" Damon suggested, opening the gate for her.

"I hope she likes Ceddie's book," Beryl said. It might be, she thought, that the author would advise him to change the ending, as he had considered doing some weeks ago. Though she feared it was disloyal of her, she had lately conceived a preference for an alteration which would permit the noble Lord Llewellyn to win the fair Lady Frances.

"I wish I dared tell you how fetching you look today," he commented when they reached a semi-secluded spot. "But I cannot while we may be observed from the house; your blushes might shock the spinsters. I could wish these fruit trees more mature—they're not so shielding as the labyrinth at Deerhurst. Or am I supposed to refrain from remarks of that kind? I'm not perfectly sure how you expect me to behave after that pleasant interlude on the terrace."

Greatly though she was tempted, Beryl knew it would not be proper to offer any encouragement until she had broken with Peter. But he was Damon: It was entirely possible that he would need no encouragement. She met his inquiring gaze boldly, but her fingers trembled on his arm when he led her farther along the path.

"Does this silence mean you're angry with me for what happened the night of the ball? I was at fault, I acknowledge it, but you were so dazzling that I simply couldn't help myself."

"Nor I," she admitted. "And I am also to blame,

but sometimes when a gentleman begs a kiss, one complies, even if not altogether willing."

"Does one indeed?" he asked dryly. "But you were not unwilling, were you? I would have been conscious of that, and to employ the same candor you so delight in, it seemed quite otherwise to me."

"Must you pick apart everything I say?" she cried, laughing up at him. "No sooner have I made up my mind that it was simply another bit of foolishness, like that time in the labyrinth, you try to make it something more. Or less. What do you want from me, Damon?"

But when he failed to answer her, she feared her question about his intentions had displeased him. Perhaps the kiss had meant more to her than it had to Damon. He was a man of wide experience in these matters, while she was but a novice.

She was glad to see Miss Jane coming across the lawn, rescuing her from what had become a most uncomfortable situation. "We are admiring your garden," she greeted the other lady. "One quite forgets that the road is so near, your trees and hedge hide it so well!"

"My sister and I had the choosing of some of the plants, but my mother does most of the work herself," Jane replied, her eyes moving from Beryl's flushed countenance to Damon's impassive one.

"She has created a charming retreat," he said.

"Oh, yes," Beryl added, "quite charming."

Jane smiled. "I shall tell her you said so—the value of such praise is doubled when it comes from a Kinnard of Deerhurst." With a bow, Lord Elston excused himself, thereby depriving her of further observations, but she perceived that relations between this interesting couple were not so innocent as they might want her to think. And yet that didn't quite fit with what Cedric Kinnard had told her of his sister's secret engagement. "We have a bench here," she said to the self-conscious young lady. "Will you sit with me, Lady Beryl?"

When they were side by side on the garden seat, Beryl looked into the round, pleasant face of the authoress and asked bluntly, "What do you think of Ceddie's book, ma'am? Will he be able to publish it?"

"Oh yes, I expect so. I'm favorably impressed by what I've seen, and apart from a few over-worn expressions and one questionable plot contrivance, it is a highly original work. I'm a great reader of novels, quite apart from writing them, and flatter myself that I am something of a judge. He wants to send the book to the Minerva Press, but in my opinion it deserves a wider and more discerning audience than bored young ladies seeking a thrill, or ignorant schoolgirls whose tastes are too erratic. I know whereof I speak, for I have grown nieces myself." She went on to describe a recent afternoon's shopping in Alton, during which she and a niece stopped at the small circulating library. "A copy of *Sense and Sensibility* lay upon the counter and while I stood by, carefully concealing my great interest, Anna took up the first volume. To my dismay as an author—and my secret amusement as her aunt—she promptly set it down again, saying she was certain of its being rubbish simply from the title! But that's Anna all over—anything smelling of sense is to be avoided, and I'm sorry to say she's no stranger to sensibility."

"I'm glad you think Ceddie shows promise as a

writer, for he is the youngest of five boys and must make his own way in the world."

Eyes dancing, Jane said, "I have five brothers myself. Not one would pattern a heroine on Cassandra or me, of that you may be sure!"

"Oh, but it was only my engagement which inspired him, not myself."

"He does have a wonderful ability to take a story from life and yet make it seem his own creation," said the authoress with a reflective air. "I don't, not very often. Nearly everything I write comes from my imagination, and only the smallest incidents are suggested to me by my own experience."

Beryl asked curiously, "Do you find greater merit in works composed purely from imagination?"

"Merit?" Jane repeated, as if struck by the question. "I never considered it, but any work bearing a resemblance to the world as it really is has merit. From my brief reading of parts of your brother's novel, I can guess it mirrors life at Deerhurst, but if some characters are drawn from people he knows, it is just as clearly a work of fiction."

"Did you like the ending?"

"Do you?" The young lady flinched, and prosaic Jane, no friend to sentiment and seldom in sympathy with lovelorn young ladies, patted Beryl's hand. "I approve of a happy ending, which is certainly the best kind." In fact, she had recognized that the novel's resolution was its only serious flaw, but she knew herself to be exacting and occasionally unconventional in her requirements. The public would no doubt be content, which was just as well. Mr. Kinnard had been adamant in his defense of the final chapter. Privately, however, Jane wished Lady Beryl a less commonplace fate than that of the fictitious female she had inspired.

Their discussion of Cedric's novel was interrupted by the arrival of Jane's friend Martha Lloyd, who walked around from the bakehouse, a pair of dogs dancing at her heels, and invited them inside for tea.

"Well!" said Cassandra Austen a little while later, when she and Jane and Martha stood at the window waving goodbye to the company. "A marquis, no less! Our mother *will* be sorry she was indisposed today. And you, Jane, sitting in the garden with an earl's daughter all this while—we've come up in the world with a vengeance!"

"Such a pretty creature," murmured Miss Lloyd, watching as Lord Elston tenderly handed the object of her admiration into his curricle.

"She is," Jane agreed. She had noted, as her sister and friend had not, the cool look Lady Beryl had given the marquis when he handed her into the curricle. Here was a tale every bit as intriguing as one of her own devising: a lovely young girl, engaged to one lover, separated from him and thrown into the company of an excessively handsome and personable nobleman. She hoped with all her heart that Lady Beryl would win the gentleman of her dreams, whichever he might be.

"I wonder, will we often have hordes of people descending upon our humble door now that you're a literary lioness, Jane?" asked Martha, smiling up at her taller friend.

Before the authoress could reply, her sister said emphatically, "I hope not. It wouldn't do for us at all."

"I predict that today's visitors, the first of their kind, will also be the last." Jane tapped her chin several times in a thoughtful manner, then turned from the window abruptly, sitting down at the table on which was spread her work in progress. Cassandra and Martha crept out of the room, leaving her in peace, and she forgot the events of the day as she returned to the pleasant task of knocking *Pride and Prejudice* into shape.

# 10

*No, I sho'd think, that marriage might,*
*Rather than mend, put out the light.*
— ROBERT HERRICK

Not far from the fishing village of Selsey stood a windmill, and one afternoon a convivial party from Deerhurst gathered there to share a picnic. They dined on cold meats, cheese, bread and fruit, washing down their humble meal with an excellent vintage purloined from Lord Rowan's cellars. Afterward Cedric, careless of his garb, lay down on the grass to read; the others, seated on cushions, conversed languidly as heavy clouds rolled in from the sea. The forthcoming change in the weather made the carriage horses and hacks stamp and snort and toss their heads in warning.

Charlotte, frowning at her sated and idle companions, said briskly, "I thought we would walk along the beach. Beryl lured me here with a tale of having found a Roman coin in the vicinity."

"That was at Selsey Bill," said Beryl, twirling the ferrule of a sunshade which resembled a yellow tulip turned upside down.

"Well, can't we at least tour the village?"

"It isn't very pretty," Louisa said without stirring from her semi-recumbent position.

Her husband, however, was not averse to a change of scenery. "We'll have to move soon enough; there's rain in the air. Sid, Damon, take Beryl and Miss Selby down to the sea for a quick look, while we older folk repair to an inn."

"Poor Louisa," Beryl teased, "wed to such a graybeard."

Damon, helping her to her feet, said, "Roger, you'd best not age too quickly. Sid and I are your contemporaries, and we're not in our dotage yet. He is right, though, Louisa—you'll be more comfortable indoors, and Ceddie won't care where he lands. Where shall we meet?"

"At the Dolphin," answered Roger promptly. "I want your opinion of the ale they brew there."

So Beryl and her brother and Damon and his cousin joined the oystercatchers and seagulls scavenging along the shoreline. Charlotte kept her eyes carefully trained to the sands beneath her feet, hoping for the sight of some stray piece of antiquity, and Sidney steered her away from the water's edge whenever she wandered too close. Soon they were far behind Beryl and Damon, whose promenade to the village was the swifter.

"I fear your day will be spoilt if you fail to find treasure," Sidney commented. "I ought to have borrowed my sister's Roman coin to drop in your path."

Poking at the shingle with the point of Beryl's sunshade, she replied, "My day certainly won't be spoilt—nothing could do that. Do you know, I used to think the country the dullest of places and would never have believed that I might one day set about ruining my best half-boots with sand and salt water!"

"Are your feet wet?" he asked in sudden concern.

"Not even damp. I was only jesting."

"I wish you wouldn't . . . jest, I mean. Not now, when there's so much else we might say to one another."

Charlotte looked at him curiously, for the substance and tone of this remark differed greatly from the lighthearted banter that he had hitherto addressed to her. "You must be aware, Captain Kinnard, that I've been flirting with you since I came to Deerhurst. It is a shallow exercise, an old habit that I can't seem to shake off, except with Damon."

Sidney, a little pale beneath his Peninsular tan, said gently, "Charlotte, you can't convince me this is merely a flirtation."

The rising wind which had ruffled her escort's brown hair whipped at her skirts. "Oh, very well," she said, "it is rather more, but what does it signify? I'm not on the catch for a husband."

"Nor I for a wife."

"I didn't think you were."

"With Tracy's wedding and my sister Beryl pledged, Cupid has wrought havoc amongst Kinnard hearts of late." Reaching for her hand, he asked, "Would you refuse me if I dropped to my knees here in the sand and begged you to be kind to a lovesick soldier?"

"How can I say?" she answered impatiently. "I do value my new-won independence, for my aunt's legacy permits me to enjoy the luxury of being twenty-seven, unwed, and unpromised. I might like following the drum, though, and I'm sure I want to know you better before some bullet catches you. But," she concluded, "if I married, it would please my mother too much, and that I cannot bring myself to do!"

He was unsure whether she was teasing or had spoken in earnest. "I wouldn't want you to follow the drum," he stated flatly. "It's not at all romantic and a hellish life for any woman, whether an officer's wife or a foot-soldier's doxy. War is nothing like the stirring parades and fine military reviews you may have witnessed. One day I shall tire of it, but not till we've taught Boney a lesson."

"And after you've beaten him, will you then retire on half-pay and take up residence in Bath, or some suitably dull town? Will you be a crusty old general in need of a companion?"

He laughed and reached for Charlotte's hand again, swinging it back and forth as he said gaily, "Oh, it won't take as long as that to bring down the eagle! And I'll not be crusty, my girl, nor would I ever consent to living in Bath—too stodgy for me! No, I'll go to London straightaway and seek out a certain pair of black eyes, and then— who can say?"

Charlotte laughed with him, her pale complexion greatly improved by her blushes. "Oh, but this is the strangest conversation! Are you trifling with me?"

Sidney answered this charge by carrying her hand to his lips.

While Miss Selby and Captain Kinnard discussed the future in their oblique fashion, Beryl and Damon had reached the small harbor. The tide was coming in, and the waves lapped at the few dilapidated fishing vessels which bobbed at their moorings. All were half-decked and a little more than twenty feet long, with low sterns to accommodate trawling, and Beryl explained that these were known as Selsey smacks. "They're mostly used for lobstering," she informed him. "The richest beds are out at Owers Shoal, just off the coast."

By the time it began to drizzle Damon had given up on his cousin and her swain and suggested they join Roger and Louisa at the inn. But Beryl suddenly gasped, as if in horror, and when he looked at her inquiringly, she cried out, "My shawl!"

"What?"

"My shawl," she repeated wildly. "What happened to it? Did I drop it on the beach? But I couldn't have done that without knowing."

"Perhaps your sister has it," he suggested.

"No, no, I remember now. I cast it aside because I was so warm in the sun, and it must still be lying in the grass. It's green and yellow, in a paisley pattern, which accounts for my not noticing it. What a stupid thing to do! The rain will surely ruin it."

What had formerly been a gentle sea breeze was now a fierce gale, and the raindrops were falling mercilessly. Damon cared nothing for the fate of the shawl but a great deal for the young lady, so he went with her across the wasteland, thinking they could at least seek shelter inside the mill. But there was no sign of the miller or his boy now, and the door was locked.

Beryl found her lost property and used it to cover her head, although the silk flowers on her bonnet were already soaked.

Above the raging wind Damon shouted, "We must get out of the rain! Is there some other house nearby?"

Nodding vigorously, she answered, "The cottage—come, it's not far."

He took her hand, and together they ran as

swiftly as Beryl could manage in her long skirts, both laughing as the rain lashed their faces. Standing at the edge of the marsh was a solitary, weatherbeaten dwelling; a watermark along its outer walls was indicative of past floods. When they reached its door Beryl knocked timidly, but Damon knew no such polite hesitation, and shoved it open unceremoniously, pulling her in after him.

The room's only source of light was a single window with panes obscured by grime and cobwebs, and for a moment they stood panting, breathless from their mad dash, waiting for their eyes to grow accustomed to the darkness. There was one piece of furniture, a long trestle table set against one wall. Sailcloth and fishing nets were heaped upon the floor, and there was a pervasive odor of rotting wood and salt marsh. "I'm not surprised to find this place uninhabited," Damon commented. "Whose is it?"

"Once it belonged to a fisherman, but now it serves as the Rowleys' hiding place. They keep their—their goods here." When he grimaced, she said tartly, "At least we're out of the rain."

At that moment an ominous stream of water poured from above, splattering onto the floor. "Are we?" he asked pithily. He moved to the pile of sailcloth and lifted a portion to disclose a dozen or more bottles lying side by side in a neat row. "I hope your friends won't mind if I sample their goods while we wait out the storm," he said over his shoulder as he fashioned a makeshift couch from the heavy canvas. "Come and sit," he invited her when he was done. "Are you thoroughly drenched?"

"Not down to my petticoats." She untied the ribbons of her bonnet and set it on the floor. "My shawl kept most of the rain off," she said, snuggling deeper into the nest of sailcloth.

"No more about that plaguey shawl, if you please!" He removed his coat and placed it around her shoulders.

"Do you suppose Sid and Charlotte reached the inn before the storm broke? They must wonder what became of us—and Louisa will be so worried."

Her innocent remark had disturbing implications, and Damon ran his hand through his hair distractedly before answering. "They'll expect us to take refuge in some local house, suitably chaperoned by the fisherman, his wife, and at least six children for good measure. Which story you'll encourage your brother to accept, my girl, for I don't fancy meeting him—or your parent—at twenty paces. Now then, shall we try this nectar of the gods?" It took but a moment to dislodge the seal, whereupon he took one long sniff and said blissfully, "Cherry brandy. This will warm you, *petite*, if you don't object to drinking it straight from the bottle." He pressed it into Beryl's cold hands, and when she showed hesitation said teasingly, "Never fear, I won't make you drunk."

She lifted the bottle to her lips and took a tentative sip, then made a face. "Horrid stuff—it tastes like medicine."

He took the bottle from her. "All the more for me, then. Are you comfortable?"

"Yes, quite."

Damon leaned his back against the wall and stretched out his long legs. Staring up at the sagging roofbeams, he murmured, "How quiet it is, except for the rain. I can even hear what you're thinking."

Laughing softly, she said, "I won't allow that to be possible."

"Oh no? The thoughts are whirling fast and furiously: 'What will I do if he tries to kiss me? What if he makes improper advances?'"

She choked. "I was thinking no such thing!"

"Then you are very foolish and just as ignorant, for this is precisely the sort of situation that often figures in the dreams of a debauched gentleman like myself. No one is near to save you or to stop me." He took one of her long curls in his hand, then dropped it with a regretful sigh.

At the sound of a particularly loud thunderclap, Beryl turned to him and said fretfully, "It's raining harder now."

He pulled her close, intending to provide comfort, but something akin to intoxication or insanity—or both—obtruded. And because it was invitation and not protest he read in her dilated eyes, he cradled her face in his palms and printed a kiss upon her curving lips. They were soft and yielding, and he found that he could not stop.

Beryl melted into his arms, twining herself about his hard-muscled form. She didn't shrink when he pressed her to the floor, or when his mouth left hers and teased her earlobe before tracing a line from her chin to the column of her throat. Although she knew she ought to push his hands away, she submitted to his caresses, and when he kissed her again, she rendered up her very soul. She was giddy with longing, drunk with desire, and entirely unashamed of her wanton response to his lovemaking. And only when his arms suddenly went slack and he lifted his head to look at her did her euphoria give way to panic.

Divested of his coat, with his hair mussed by

wind and rain and her fingers, he looked much younger and more vulnerable. His expression was grave, and his voice was still husky with passion when he said, "This is madness."

"If so, it is a delicious kind of madness."

Smiling faintly, he asked, "Don't you know what I came so close to doing?" He pulled up her drooping sleeve, his fingers lingering at her shoulder. "Skin so soft, lips so sweet—you were nearly my downfall, Beryl."

"But what is wrong?" she asked him. "Did I displease you? Do you prefer ladies who shrink and slap and cry out that they will not? You know I have no experience in these matters."

"Well, you won't be getting any from me," he said, abruptly climbing to his feet. "I would never take you here, not in a place like this. So fine a creature deserves the stateliest bed, the gentle glow of a fire to enhance your charms, and above all, a wedding ring upon your finger."

Beryl untangled her legs from the heavy canvas and followed him. "Then take me as your wife, Damon."

He appeared to be startled and not entirely pleased, and he didn't reply immediately. "Marriage is your destiny, not mine."

A moment ago he had been kissing her ardently; now he was remote and passionless. Had her impetuous proposal shocked him so much? "I believed you cared for me," she said simply, by way of explanation.

"I do, Beryl, but I never meant for things to go this far, I swear it. It seems I am unable to control myself." With a ghost of a smile, he added, "You make it very difficult."

She regarded him silently, uncertainly, waiting

for him to say something that would make her
grounded hopes take flight again.

"To my profound and sincere regret, I cannot
make you an offer," he went on. "You must know
why. Surely you've heard about my parents, and
how they met their end?"

"Yes," she whispered, wondering what the dead
past had to do with this dismal present.

"But of course," he said with a shrug, "the
whole world knows at least one version of the
story. Who told you?"

"Louisa, soon after you came to Deerhurst."

He took a single step toward her, then he was
still. "Imagine if you can, you are so well-loved, a
child with a cold, unfeeling father. A little boy
who hears the servants whispering that his mother
is a stablehand's doxy." His eyes narrowed to blue
slits. "And she was. I don't blame her—my father
drove her to it, in driving her away. I found her
journal among her effects, so I know she *was* carrying a child at the time of the accident. Rumor
does not always lie. It's just as well that she died
as she did, for I don't doubt my father would have
killed her, once he learned of her condition."

"That is sad—nay, tragic—but what does it have
to do with you and me?"

"To put it plainly, my great-grandmother, that
beautiful Swedish countess who graced the English King's court, was a bitch with an ice-bound
heart, and she spawned a line of devils. Her son
and her grandson, my father, were notorious for
their cruelty, their vices, their unnatural—"

"But you are not as they were," Beryl protested.

"You say so only because I've been on my best
behavior, which is hardly to my credit. Lulling
the victim into a sense of false security is a time-

honored seducer's trick. So you see, I am a true Lovell after all, and as such incapable of the devotion you crave, the affection—the constancy. The love." She winced, but he continued mercilessly, "Ask Charlotte if you don't believe me. She can describe my sins to you in great detail, and she knows why I will never marry."

"Never? But what of your title, and Elston Towers? What about family duty?"

He waved these considerations aside. "I have no family to speak of. I'm the last of my line, and the title will die with me—which is just as well, in my opinion. As for the estate, when I have gone to my reward, or my punishment, Roger will have Elston Towers. He has even agreed to add the Lovell name to his own. My lawyer drew up the necessary papers last week, they've been signed and sealed and attached to the new will which names him my heir." He walked over to her and gazed down into her wide, unhappy eyes. "I have been toying with you, Beryl, and I'm truly sorry for it. We might know great joy together, wed or unwed, but one day it would end, and in a way far more unpleasant for you than for me. No woman has ever held my interest for very long. You'll be much happier with your Mr. Yeates, who is worthy of your good faith and gentle kisses. I'd make a very poor husband for a girl like you, and besides, you always preferred me as a friend, remember?"

There was no point in explaining that she no longer had any intention of marrying Peter, nor could she answer his arguments against matrimony. If he loved her he wouldn't have rejected her love. It was that simple.

Determined to show him a brave face, she lifted her chin, and her voice was almost steady when she said, "The rain has stopped. I think we'd better go now."

"You aren't concerned that I've compromised you, I hope?"

"Oh, no," she answered. "And I'll support whatever story you tell to excuse our absence to Louisa and Sid." She crossed the room to retrieve her bonnet and placed it upon her dishevelled head, then wrapped herself up in the green and yellow shawl. Inside she was slowly dying. He had shoved her aside, dismissing her just as he would a troublesome and overly affectionate puppy. Spurned by the man she loved, she was still pledged to one she hardly knew: Could anything be more unfair?

A moment later she followed him blindly into the sodden grayness, leaving the secret of her shattered faith and short-lived dreams hidden away in the deserted cottage.

Beryl never completely remembered the rest of that afternoon, nor did Damon ever forget it.

The tale he told about taking refuge with a cottager on the edge of the village was readily accepted as the truth. During the drive back to Deerhurst he rode beside the landau, watching Louisa chafe her sister's hands, which she declared were cold as ice. Beryl was decidedly pale and strangely subdued, and he felt like a monster for treating her so unkindly. And when the cavalcade drew up before the house, he slipped away unnoticed, for everyone else was assisting her out of the carriage.

To the Kinnards' surprise and dismay, their father had returned during their excursion, and his massive figure filled up the doorway.

"What's amiss?" Lord Rowan boomed as his

children trooped guiltily into the great hall. Peering into Beryl's strained face, he said, "Poor puss, you don't look at all well."

She smiled up at him wanly. "I'm tired, that's all."

Glowering at the others, he demanded to know what had happened.

"We had a picnic at Selsey, and Beryl was caught in the rain," his elder daughter replied. "But you needn't worry, Papa, she'll have a warm bath at once and I'll put her to bed afterwards." As the earl began shouting for fires to be lit and kettles boiled, she hurried Beryl toward the staircase, pausing only to whisper a plea to Miss Selby. "I beg you, do what you can to divert our father, otherwise he'll expire from an apoplexy. He's always at his most irrational when Beryl is feeling poorly."

His lordship had remained in the hall, pacing and blustering, and Charlotte surmised that poor Sidney had made a mull of his explanations. As the earl castigated his favorite son as a careless guardian of his sister's welfare, she wished Damon had not disappeared. Thrusting herself between Sidney and his irate parent, she said, "Lord Rowan, will you come for a stroll in the gardens with me? After the rain, the scent of the roses will be divine!"

He said distractedly, "Oh, aye, the roses. Sid, take Miss Selby outside, there's a good fellow."

But Sidney, correctly interpreting Charlotte's shake of the head as an appeal for refusal, encouraged his father to go with her, adding, "You can see Beryl after she has been made comfortable."

As new fears surfaced, his lordship's fury was forgotten, and he said brokenly, "Poor child, did you see how white she was? We lost your mother this way—a chill, caught in the damp. It settled on her lungs."

"I doubt that your daughter is in any danger, my lord," Charlotte said in a soothing voice. "Damon kept her out of the rain as best he could, and she never got very wet. Warm broth and a hot brick will do wonders for her, you'll see."

He said he hoped she was right, and after she coaxed him a bit more he agreed to go with her.

The rose garden was as sweet-scented as Charlotte had prophesied, but her reluctant escort took no notice of his surroundings. "Louisa will know what to do," he said as though trying to convince himself, "she's clever about making possets and whatnot. Beryl is better at nursing sick animals— she has cured foals and lambs and squirrels by the score." He lapsed into silence.

Charlotte asked about his stay in London, but this was not an auspicious topic. "The damned place was as tiresome as ever," the earl responded. "And Tracy was no great companion. I was glad when he left me to stay with his godfather in Kent. He was making my life a misery, always talking of that Yeates fellow. I hope to hear no more of *him* now I'm home again."

"Is your lordship still so disturbed by that affair? I think you need not be."

"You lack my perspective, young woman, that's why," he retorted. "If Beryl had wanted to wed some steady lad she'd known all her life, at least I might bestow her hand with an easy mind. But no, my soft-hearted little girl has to fancy herself in love with the first gentleman who made up to her." He began pacing the plot of grass on which they stood until Charlotte expected him to wear it down to a dirt track before her eyes.

"It may not be my place to say so, but a prudent father would have thrown her into Mr. Yeates's company, counting upon time to reveal his faults."

"Are you criticizing my management of my family?"

"With a daughter one whit less dutiful than Lady Beryl, you'd have been forced to countenance an elopement long ere this. Have I permission to speak frankly, sir?" The earl signified assent. "I truly believe Mr. Yeates is the least of your troubles. Your daughter wasn't well acquainted with him, and one cannot love at a distance for very long." Her black eyes softened as she added speculatively, "Or only in very rare cases. Lord Rowan, if you could but bring yourself to accept the inevitability of her marriage, you might look much higher than a mere Mr. Yeates. Nor need you look very far."

The earl stopped short. "What are you suggesting?"

"What would you say to Damon as a prospective son-in-law?" she asked him.

He stopped treading the ground long enough to consider this. "I can't see any reason to oppose such a match, but neither can I force it on my girl. In one sense it would be just as unequal a marriage as the one with Yeates. My puss has little knowledge of the world, especially Elston's world. He has sophisticated tastes, and I expect he would be impatient with her simple country ways."

"I don't think she'd mind." With a saucy smile, Charlotte added, "You are not precisely a man of easy temper yourself."

"No. No, I'm not," he agreed with some pride.

Wagging his head at her, he said, "You, miss, are a minx, but I can see you're a wise woman, for all your nonsense. If she thought she might be happy with young Damon, if he could woo her out of this infatuation with Yeates, I'd give him my blessing."

Only a short time later he had reason to be grateful to Miss Selby for opening his eyes, for no sooner did they return to the house than Lord Elston requested a private interview.

A single glance at the young man's white, resolute face told the whole story, and recalled to the earl an ordeal he'd suffered decades ago, when he'd sought permission to wed a duke's daughter. Hoping to put the aspirant at ease, Lord Rowan invited Damon into his bookroom and offered him a glass of wine. To his surprise, it was politely declined.

"I'm glad you returned today, sir, that I might offer my thanks for your hospitality these past weeks," Damon began. "Although my invitation came from Louisa, all of your family have exerted themselves to make my stay here most enjoyable."

"It has been our pleasure." Yes, Lord Rowan thought exultantly, young Damon would do: He had a title and a fortune, and there was liking on both sides. If his precious child must marry, better it should be to the marquis than that brash commoner from the north. But this hesitation, while not unusual for a young fellow in love, was irksome to one as impatient as the earl. "You haven't sought me out merely to say how much you are enjoying your visit, of that I am certain."

"No," Damon replied. "My purpose is to inform you, most regretfully, that I shall be leaving Deerhurst tomorrow."

# 11

*How ill doth he deserve a Lover's name.*
—THOMAS CAREW

As Damon drove his curricle along the dusty road to Brighton, he was blind to the beauties of the downland, dappled by sun and shadow. When he crossed the River Arun, he was so preoccupied with the trouble which had sent him bolting from Deerhurst that he was only peripherally aware of the looming castle beside the bridge.

His behavior of the previous day was indefensible. He had always known how impressionable and innocent Beryl was, and therefore he had been wrong to arouse her passions. If she hated him, it was no more than he deserved.

What a fool he had been to tumble into love with his virginal charmer, who, like any romantic-minded schoolgirl, believed kissing and cuddling implied an intention to wed. Though he might have entered into matrimony with the best of good intentions, it would have required him to make promises he could never hope to keep, and the result would be a lifetime of sorrow and regret for both of them. Oh, there would be delight in the beginning, but in time marriage, even to Beryl, might grow as stale as his less durable arrangements with his mistresses. If he treated her coldly, or sought other companions, she would deem it her failure. Like his mother, she might console herself with a lover and meet with similar disaster. Yes, he told himself, she would do much better to wed Mr. Yeates than to shackle herself to a cold-hearted marquis who was uncertain of his ability to make her—and himself—happy.

Having settled her fate in his mind, he considered his own future. A few weeks at Brighton would surely help him to recover his spirits, and the sudden change of plan was made simpler by the fact that each year he engaged a set of rooms at the inn adjoining the Regent's grandiose Royal Pavilion. The popularity of the seaside resort had grown since his first visit years ago, so he was not dismayed to find its streets crowded by visitors, even though the person they most wanted to see was not yet in residence at his summer palace, now embellished with fanciful cupolas and turrets.

That evening Damon set out for the Old Ship assembly rooms, where he was reunited with several acquaintances. The Wainworths and Lady Martha Onslow greeted him with an ostentatious demonstration of delight. Mr. Davenant Hughes was there, and also a blond female wearing cream satin and pearls, who met Damon's eyes in a long glance of mutual recognition and appraisal.

Noting this exchange, Lady Wainworth murmured, "Georgiana has been asking me about your rift with Eliza Preston, but I was unable to enlighten her."

"Don't tell me Eliza is here, too," he muttered.

"Oh no, she managed to find consolation elsewhere. And perhaps you'll be the one to console our poor Georgiana, whose latest flirt has deserted her. I must say, she has the worst luck with men."

Damon knew the truth of it far better than Lady Wainworth. Georgiana had, at various times in her checkered past, been involved with Dominic Blythe, and after him Ramsey Blythe, Justin's late and unlamented elder brother. She was the relict of Sir Algernon Titus, who had survived his duel with Dominic only to die at the hands of his own physician. After serving as the unfortunate baronet's second, Damon had also befriended the widow—which was more than Ramsey, her jealous lover, had done. In recent years they had sometimes met socially, and the last time had been the night before he'd left London for Deerhurst, when she had shared his box at the opera.

Making his way to her side, he reflected that at least there was no need to feign delight at seeing her again.

Georgiana smiled up at him as she said, "I would swear the musicians paused for a fraction of a second when you entered the room, they were so amazed—as are we all. Has your lordship wearied of country life at last?"

"Most things pall with time," he answered carelessly. "And you, my dear, did you come to Brighton unescorted this year?"

"Dear me, no. Though I might as well have done, because my friend had to return to town. Such a bore."

He perceived her reluctance to discuss whatever had happened and willingly let the subject drop. As he listened to her description of the Wainworths' latest marital squabble, it occurred to him that admitting this ravishing creature to his bed might alleviate the pain of parting from Beryl

Kinnard. Georgiana was in every way her opposite: tall, with an abundance of rich, golden hair,
she was endowed with a magnificently lush figure.
He had always liked her; given her history, she
had experience enough to recommend her. Best of
all, she wouldn't make excessive demands upon
him. Damon immediately engaged her for the next
set of dances, and afterwards invited her to join
him at the theater later in the week.

For the next fortnight he provided his friends
with a new interest, following the progress of
courtship of the fair widow. But for some reason
Damon was not as eager to be done with the pre-
liminaries as he'd been with other prospective
mistresses; in fact, he found himself drawing them
out to hitherto unprecedented lengths. And although he stayed out late each night, he invariably
returned to his rooms at the Castle Inn, where,
brandy glass in hand, he would reminisce about a
long chain of golden summer days, of the idyll
which had begun the moment Lady Beryl Kinnard
had stepped across the threshold of the drawing
room at Deerhurst and into his life. To dwell upon
her winning ways was pointless now that he was
done with her, and he derived little real pleasure
from reliving the shared jokes and games, the
horseback rides, rehearsals for the concert, their
first sweet kiss in the gardens—and those last ones
in that cottage on the marsh. The final step in this
rite of self-torture was to summon up her shocked
face as it had looked when he refused to marry
her.

Never in his life had he envied his best friend
Dominic and his dear cousin Justin so very much.

Dominic had met his Nerissa only hours after
his duel with Sir Algernon, and she supported him

through a painful period of exile which had ended in an inquest. Doubts and suspicions had plagued Justin and Miranda throughout their rocky courtship and had followed them to the altar and beyond. Yet both couples had survived the obstacles fate had placed in their way, emerging from their many trials strengthened, their marriages intact.

But he was not so brave as Dominic, nor so patient as Justin. He was hedonistic, cynical, spoiled, and selfish—altogether wrong for a sweet and uncomplicated girl like Beryl.

Ultimately he had to acknowledge to himself that he had no inclination to ravish the ravishing Georgiana. Nor did he lust after the pretty little actress at the New Theater who smiled up at his box so provocatively, and in whose eyes he read an open invitation. He doubted the ability of any female to comfort him in his present state of despondency, other than the one he could not have. For Beryl he suffered no lack of desire. If he had taken her on that crude bed of sailcloth, he would never have been free. He would have been obliged to marry her, like it or not, and might that not be better than his present anguished unfulfillment?

He thought about her constantly, wondering how she was passing her days and nights. He imagined her clipping roses, practicing on the pianoforte in the drawing room, humming a gay tune as she weeded her lavender beds. He'd loved to watch her playing with her nephews, and from all he had observed, she seemed destined to make a fine mother. No doubt Mr. Yeates would know great pleasure in providing her with a family.

But where was Yeates? In all this time, Damon had not seen him nor heard him mentioned by any of his acquaintance.

Lady Beryl's betrothed was absent from all the fashionable assemblies and never showed his face at Raggett's club. One night at the play, Damon took advantage of the interval to ask Georgiana if she had met a Peter Yeates during her stay in Brighton. When she colored up and began fanning herself frantically, he regarded her with greater interest than he had displayed of late and said, "You do know him."

"I thought I did," she replied bitterly.

"Oh? I don't mean to pry, but I wish you would explain what you mean."

"He is the gentleman who accompanied me here." While Damon digested this, Georgiana continued her agitated play with her fan. "We met during the Season, at a time when I was in desperate straits. Algy didn't leave me very much, you know, so I have a habit of attaching myself to handsome young men with deep pockets. When the rent on my house in Clifford Street came due last quarter, Peter Yeates was kind enough to lend me a sum of money. That is, he let me have it in exchange for . . . well, I'm sure you can guess. Not long after, we came to Brighton together and took a house in the Marine Parade."

Damon, clenching his gloved hands, said grimly, "And then he deserted you."

She confirmed it, adding, "He left for London a fortnight ago. If he intended to break with me, he concealed the truth. I knew only that he wished to visit his bankers. Now his Brighton creditors have begun dunning me, and I expect I'll have to move from the Marine Parade to a cheaper lodging."

"No, you won't. I'll give you some money. But," he added swiftly, meeting her eyes, "I shan't de-

mand the same form of repayment Yeates did. I've
no right to be repaid in any case, for I still consider myself in debt to *you*, Georgiana. I haven't
forgotten that you stepped forward to save my
friend Dominic's neck, all those years ago, at some
cost to yourself. I know you suffered by it, though
not as much as my cousin Ramsey."

"I couldn't stand by and let Nick be destroyed
by a vindictive lie. A lifetime ago, before I was
married, he brought me to Brighton for a very gay
time. And afterwards I had no regrets—not as I do
now."

Damon scarcely heard this plaintive remark, for
he was looking back to the day he'd arrived at
Deerhurst, and Beryl's joy at receiving her first
letter from her beloved. And all this time the
damned fellow had been consorting with another
woman!

What manner of man could betray Beryl? He
had certainly been unable to do it, and with far
less to bind him to her than a promise of marriage.
But, he wondered, what were Yeates's intentions
now? A gentleman did not break an engagement—
but, of course, the difficulty was that he'd already
proved himself to be no gentleman, first by slight-
ing Beryl, and now by abandoning Georgiana.

In the morning he ordered his valet to pack his
bags, and less than an hour after rising he took up
the reins of his curricle and set out along the New
Road to London. The Wainworths had bidden him
to a party in honor of Lady Martha Onslow's
birthday, but he must depend on Georgiana to
convey his excuses and regrets. He had business
in town.

He knew the turnpike well, for he'd raced it in
his younger days and had won, but not even then

had he been in such a fever of impatience. At the half-way house in Horley he paced the yard while waiting for the ostler to harness a fresh team, chafing at a delay of only a few minutes. At Croyden, when he consulted his watch, he smiled for the first time all day, knowing he would reach Westminster Bridge in two hours. He had surpassed his own record.

Damon's first view of church steeples and cathedral spires was obscured by coal smoke, but as he crossed the Thames he felt a tangible sense of homecoming. His beloved city was as busy and bustling as ever, and though her more genteel inhabitants had removed to the seaside or the country, the humbler classes seldom deserted her. His progress to Berkeley Square was impeded by hackneys, chaises, and carriers' carts, and when he finally reached Mayfair he noted that a number of door knockers had been removed, including the one on Elston House.

The butler did not appear to be startled when he opened the front door to his master, but two footmen in their shirtsleeves stared as he stepped into the hall. Mimms, removing his lordship's driving coat, issued a curt order to his underlings to remove the holland covers in the upstairs rooms at once.

"Just so," Damon said approvingly. "And, Mimms, you may inform Henri that I'll be dining out tonight." Sorting through the pile of calling cards on the hall table, he asked, "Are so many people still in town?"

"Those were left immediately after your departure, my lord; there are also some letters in the library. Viscount Cavender and his lady called last week. I believe they are still staying at Solway

House, with her ladyship's cousin." The butler smiled when he said, "Permit me to say how happy I am that you are back in London, my lord."

A short time later, Damon sat down in his favorite chair to sift through those letters which had not been redirected to Deerhurst or Brighton, mostly invitations to lavish entertainments, all long past. There were a few personal notes of more recent date: A friend suggested that they make up a party for the York Races, and a querulous missive from a disagreeable aunt implored him to propose her ambitious son for membership to White's. A brief epistle from his agent informed him that the hay had been cut and the sheep shorn at Elston Towers, and did his lordship plan to inspect his property in the near future? Damon tossed this letter aside, for he never troubled himself about estate business and saw no need to begin now. But he would definitely attend the August Meeting at York.

Perhaps there he could throw off this fit of ennui which had prevented him from taking his usual pleasure from Brighton, beautiful ladies, and yes, even food.

That night he set out for St. James. He didn't really expect to find Peter Yeates in any of the gentlemen's clubs, nor did he, and while some of the gentlemen he met professed to know the young man, none could recall when they had last seen him, or with what fair female.

"Is he in town again?" asked one. "I saw him in Brighton a few weeks ago, cozying up to the Titus woman. Before that he was dangling after Lady Letitia Bevins. Devil of a ladies' man, Yeates."

"So I've heard," Damon responded with heavy sarcasm.

He made a tour of all the clubs on both sides of the street, and was able to determine that his quarry had been living on the fringe of high society, not quite within its bounds, making him all the more difficult to trace. He had evidently given up his former lodging in Duke Street, and no longer frequented the theaters.

The following day, while strolling along Bond Street, he was fortunate enough to meet his cousin, Lord Cavender. "Hullo there, Justin!" he cried. "Are you still in London at this benighted season?"

The viscount smiled. "I'm just as surprised to find you here, for I believed you to be quite settled in the country. Give me your arm to White's." When Damon fell into step beside him, Justin told him, "That genial old ogre Rowan was in town a few weeks ago, with Tracy in tow. Now that the Army has one less Kinnard swelling its ranks, I suppose the rest of the lads will have to fight a bit harder. What other news from Deerhurst?"

"No great deal. It was at Brighton that the scandal-broth was brewing." By the time they reached White's Club, Damon had exhausted his small collection of *on-dits*.

They took possession of a table in the new bow window where they could spy on the passersby, and after the serving-man brought wine and cheese, Damon bemoaned his lack of success in locating Peter Yeates.

"What's your interest in this fellow?" his cousin asked.

"He's engaged to Lady Beryl Kinnard."

"Is he indeed? I heard nothing about it when we were in Sussex."

"No, Lord Rowan won't permit anyone to mention the gentleman's name. He hasn't given his consent." Damon gazed thoughtfully into his glass, then drained it. "What do you know about Yeates?"

"Not a great deal, I'm afraid. He sprang up overnight, like the mushroom I suspect he is. He goes to the best tailors, drives a team you wouldn't blush to own, and tools about in a bang-up curricle. He's a great topic of conversation, though— the other day someone was telling me about his women, expensive ones, too. First an opera dancer, then an actress, and lately a certain widow of our mutual acquaintance. And he's a gamester. I wouldn't blame the Kinnards if they balk at the match. It's not one I'd want for my sister or daughter, especially one as unworldly as Lady Beryl."

"Nor I!"

If the viscount wondered at his cousin's vehemence, he showed no sign of it. "The company Yeates keeps is very much below your touch, but I can tell you that he's a regular visitor to a certain hell not far from where we sit—Number Five, Pickering Place."

"You should never have given up the spying game," Damon said, smiling across the table at his relative.

Justin leaned forward to add, "I suspect it would take a dowry many times the size of the Kinnard girl's to get him out of debt, and someone should intervene before it's too late. Rowan either can't or won't, but if he knew half of all I've told you, he'd be out of his mind."

Damon sighed heavily as he poured another glass of wine. "I've no real right to interfere. This concerns the earl, or Sidney Kinnard."

"They're not here and you are," Justin pointed out reasonably. "Besides, it wants finesse, a light touch, and no man is better at that than you. Rowan is too hotheaded, he would thunder about and make matters worse. Sidney, though more easy-tempered, is a soldier after all, and they do have a habit of solving problems at pistol point. A confrontation of that sort would be ruinous for everyone concerned. Not even my estimable cousin Dominic has lived down his duel with Sir Algernon Titus, and that was seven years ago." After a brief pause, he sighed and reported, "Nick and Nerissa are back from Jersey. Miranda had a letter from them this morning. All of a sudden she's desperate to return to Wiltshire, too, and that's why you see me here."

"I don't follow."

"We quarrelled, which is difficult to do properly in someone else's house."

"All is not bliss in the Cavender ménage?" Damon asked.

"Miranda is the light of my life, but she does have these damned variable moods—up one day, down the next. And it's worse when she's, ah, in an interesting situation."

"Is she?"

Justin nodded, and his frown was replaced by a grin. "Like a brooding hen, all she can think of is returning to her nest. We have Juliet and her nurse with us at Solway House, so Miranda has no reason not to be perfectly content, but suddenly she insists upon leaving for Cavender Chase at once—I may stay or go as I choose. If I stay, she'll never forgive me, and if I go she'll feel guilty about dragging me away. The State Opening of Parliament is a few weeks off, and I had intended to remain in London until then, if not longer."

"Go with Mira now and come back by yourself when Parliament convenes," Damon suggested.

"Perhaps I shall. When I married her, it was her ambition to be a political hostess, but nowadays she's happiest in the country. A fine Duchess of Devonshire she'd have made—her aunt wanted her to marry Hart, you know."

"She's much better off married to you."

"I'll be sure to remind her of that," Justin said on a laugh, his brown eyes bright with humor.

The new day was but an hour old when Damon entered the front room of the gaming house in Pickering Place and asked the porter to point out Mr. Yeates. "The cove in the black coat," the man said, gesturing toward the faro table.

Peter Yeates's intense concentration on the game marked him as one who played for high stakes. Because he was seated, Damon was unable to judge his height or figure, but he appeared to be of medium build. His neckcloth was elaborately tied, and Damon's sharp eyes caught the flash of a jeweled pin in the intricate folds. The face above was attractive, but the eyes were hooded by dark brows, thick and straight, which stood out starkly in the dark face and gave the young man a determined expression. He lifted his head to make some jest to his companions, and in the light of the chandelier, his thick, butter-colored hair shone like gold. But his attention never wandered from the game.

At the final turn of the card, Peter Yeates, whatever else he might be, proved that he took his losses as well as if he had a fortune to back them. Rising, he announced his intention to recoup them at *rouge et noir*, breaking off when an unknown gentleman approached.

"Mr. Yeates?" Damon asked politely, as some players dispersed and the rest settled down to the next game.

"I am."

"I'm Elston." Using Peter's ill luck as an opening gambit, Damon commiserated with him, his air that of a man who frequently rose from the table a loser, although it was untrue.

Peter's smile was a flash of white in the dark gloom. "Oh, I always land on my feet. Care to take a glass of wine with me?" Leading the way to a nearby table, he called to a waiter to bring a bottle and two glasses.

For several minutes the men conversed with the strange ease of strangers, but Peter supplied few facts about himself, confining his remarks to the present lack of entertainment to be found in London. Damon, fearing he might yet lose him to *rouge et noir*, suggested a game of piquet. They set the stakes at five shillings a point and twenty pounds on the rubber. Peter turned out to be a skillful player, but Damon matched him from the beginning and beat him in the first hand. He decided it might be a better policy to let his opponent win, knowing that no man could resist having another in his debt. During the second and third games he was so careless over discards that the young man, after winning one rubber, was emboldened to issue another challenge, and once more Damon deliberately played his worst cards.

They broached another bottle, and while Peter

filled their glasses, Damon asked offhandedly if he had wife or family in town.

"No, my lord, though parson's mousetrap will surely close upon me before the year is out."

"Permit me to felicitate you," Damon said benignly, his eyelids drooping to conceal a spark of dislike.

"And well you should, for I'll gain a fortune on my wedding day."

What was this boast? Damon wondered, for surely he knew Beryl had no such expectations. Thinking that perhaps the young man's fleeting fancy had lighted on some better-dowered lady, he prompted, "You are betrothed to an heiress?"

Peter laughed, his face flushed from wine and winning. Leaning back in his chair, he replied, "No, no, an heiress wouldn't suit my purposes. I must marry to please my grandsire, and he has his heart set on an earl's daughter. The old man is a regular Croesus, and he's so desperate to see me married into the peerage that he'll settle my debts and make me a rich man in my own right when I oblige him."

There it was, the reason this young man had courted Beryl during her visit to York. Damon wasn't even surprised that he had succeeded in winning her affections: He was personable, comely, and very, very clever. She must have been the answer to a prayer, being an earl's daughter, pretty and susceptible, and wholly ignorant of the matrimonial ambitions a wealthy merchant might have for his heir.

With a smug smile, Peter went on, "I've got myself a little beauty tucked away down in the country, safe from any poachers. Her pater is a fierce old tiger, took me into dislike the only time we met and forbade me his precious daughter. But the girl is loyal; she'll stick by me. Even so, I'm in the devil of a dilemma, for my debts have mounted up, and my grandfather is pressing me to marry her soon. It'll have to be a Gretna Green wedding, but as she's a cozy armful, it won't be too great a hardship," he concluded with a leer.

Damon, who had far better cause to know how cozy an armful Beryl was, longed to throttle the cocksure young man for bandying her name so crudely before a virtual stranger in the most hellish of London's gaming houses. Instead, he extended his card. "I am at liberty this evening, Mr. Yeates. Come to my house in Berkeley Square, for I think I might be able to help you out of these difficulties."

Moments after Peter Yeates was shown to a magnificent silk-hung drawing room, his noble host bowled him over by offering to let him have two thousand pounds.

Peter regarded the marquis in astonishment, certain that he'd misunderstood. "A loan, you mean?"

"No. Let us say a gift, with only one string attached."

The young man said ruefully, "You'll expect me to pay off my creditors."

"You may throw the money into the Thames, for all I care."

"Why do you concern yourself in *my* affairs?" Peter wondered aloud. "And to what string is your gift attached?"

"It is very simple," Damon replied. "I require

only that you release Lady Beryl Kinnard from your so-called engagement."

There was a moment of silence. "So," Peter said at last, a long, low exhalation, "last night's encounter wasn't entirely by chance. I must admit, I rather wondered at your condescension, Lord Elston."

"I expect you might indeed," Damon retorted, no longer civil. "I am a friend of the lady's family, Mr. Yeates, and recently spent two months at Deerhurst."

Peter gave a short, unpleasant laugh. "And I was right about her, wasn't I? She *is* a loyal girl, or you wouldn't try to buy me off. You may call it a gift if you choose, but I know it for a bribe. Did Rowan send you to London? Are you his errand boy?"

Damon chose to disregard this insult. "What do you say to my offer?"

"I say nothing," Peter drawled. He gazed at the marquis speculatively before saying, "Can it be that she chooses marriage to a nobody over the prospect of becoming a marchioness? How that must gall you! *And* old Rowan, for he certainly placed an appetizing fly before his little fish and must be disappointed that she failed to rise to the bait."

With difficulty, Damon refrained from boasting that Beryl had indeed risen to the lures he had cast. "What if I doubled the figure? Will you set her free in exchange for four thousand pounds?"

Peter, smiling derisively, shook his head.

"Five?"

"Not even worth my consideration."

"I'm sorry to hear it, for your acceptance of the

terms would save me and my horses a journey into Sussex. Mr. Yeates, you leave me no recourse but to hasten to Deerhurst and inform the earl that you are a gamester, deep in debt. He might also like to hear about your liaison with Georgiana Titus, and the fact that you've also been named as Lady Letitia Bevins's lover. And certainly I must consider disclosing your unfortunate taste for Covent Garden ware—I believe there was an actress, *and* an opera dancer."

A muscle jumped in Peter's cheek. "You've been very busy, haven't you, my lord. But your meddling won't serve. I mean to have the girl, and she wants to marry me."

Damon could have refuted this, but he didn't. The sensation of being slowly and inexorably backed into a corner was foreign to him, and far from agreeable. "Your engagement, such as it is, is far from being a settled thing," he pointed out. "You have no hope of securing the consent of Lady Beryl's parent, and however loyal, she is not likely to agree to an elopement." Damon smiled, sensing that he had the upper hand now. "Especially when she learns of your inconstancy."

Peter jumped to his feet, his face flushed with anger. "That ploy often has the opposite effect— Lady Beryl would think your accusations mere fabrications of a jealous man, and they could very well strengthen her resolve to wed me. If you persist in this harassment, Lord Elston, I'll be forced to demand satisfaction."

"I wish you would," Damon said mildly, "because it would save all of us a great deal of trouble. I am a modest man, so if you have any questions about my skill with a pistol, direct your inquiries to Mr. Hughes, who has seen me shoot at Manton's gallery."

The other man drew a ragged breath, then said defiantly, "I'm not afraid! If you killed me, you'd have to flee the country, and somehow I don't think that would suit you. Best have a care how you threaten me, my lord, or you may soon hear that Lady Beryl became Mrs. Yeates over the anvil at Gretna!"

"By God, I'd take her there myself to save her from *that* fate," Damon declared furiously.

"Such devotion! Tumbled her when you were at Deerhurst, did you? She looked to be ripe for it when I met her, but alas, I hadn't the opportunities you had."

Damon swung his right fist forward, connecting with the pugnacious jaw.

Peter reached out for a table to save himself from falling, but it pitched over onto the carpet, taking him down. He climbed slowly to his feet, nursing one cheek with his hand, and muttered through clenched teeth, "You'll be sorry for that, my lord."

"Begone, or I shall have you thrown into the street. It would be something of an embarrassment to you, if anyone of your near acquaintance resides in the square—which I take leave to doubt."

The young man regarded him venomously, then made an abrupt exit.

Damon, knowing he had made an enemy, flung himself into the nearest chair. Peter Yeates was everything he had feared, and worse: callous, grasping, faithless, and vicious. He cared nothing for the girl he schemed to marry, nor for poor Georgiana. Damon, comparing himself to Beryl's hero, decided that selfish though he undoubtedly was, he could lay claim to being the more honorable. But that was hardly a comfort to him as he plotted how he could be rid of the turbulent young man who might prove vindictive enough to plunge them all into scandal.

# 12

*One struggle more, and I am free*
*From pangs that rend my heart in twain;*
*One last long sigh to love and thee,*
*Then back to busy life again.*

—Lord Byron

One evening, not long after the heavy mantle of darkness had fallen upon London, a carriage halted before a house in Brook Street. Three passengers alighted: a tall, fashionably dressed lady, a lanky youth with a writing case under his arm, and a strikingly pretty young woman. The French maidservant who had ridden on the dickey snapped directions at the footman as he began unloading the baggage strapped behind.

When the three travelers entered an upstairs parlor, the solitary lady seated there looked up from her needlework to say, "Here you are at last—and after nearly three months gone! My dear Charlotte, I'd quite given up all hope of your returning to town."

Mrs. Selby had once been a handsome woman and still possessed traces of the beauty her daughter lacked, but where Charlotte's black eyes were bright and lively, the mother's were as gray and hard as agates.

Drawing her companions forward, Charlotte announced, "Here is Lady Beryl Kinnard—I trust you received my letter informing you that she will be my guest. And her brother, Mr. Kinnard, who has business in London, kindly offered us his escort."

Another gentleman had also come to town with them, but she chose to say nothing about him.

Recent developments in the Peninsula had put Sidney in a fever of impatience to rejoin his commander and his comrades, now veterans of the Battle of Salamanca. He was overjoyed that his superiors had recalled him to active service, and within a few days he would be off, carrying letters to Lord Wellington.

Charlotte had parted from her valiant soldier half an hour ago before the War Office. After promising his siblings that he would call upon them if he was able, he'd turned to her and said cheerfully, "Never fear, we'll prevail against Boney sooner or later." Reaching for her hand, he pressed it meaningfully. "Take care you don't run through that fortune of yours, my girl."

"I won't."

"Subsisting on an officer's half-pay will be no easy thing."

"Then I shall hoard my money and practice the virtues of economy in your absence."

They had revealed to no one the serious intentions that lay behind those light words, and her sweet secret would be her greatest comfort now that she had returned to her querulous mother's household.

"It is a poor time to visit London," Mrs. Selby was saying to Beryl and Cedric. "The dowagers have hardly begun to desert Worthing, and there are very few parties—so many gentlemen have gone into the country for the shooting. But not Elston," she said brightly, turning to her daughter. "He was away for the York Races but is lately returned."

"I had imagined he must be fixed in Brighton," Charlotte replied.

"Oh, he was," her mother said darkly. "You should have followed him there, Charlotte, you've always been such a good influence upon him. I can't tell you how many of my friends wrote to inform me of how very *thick* he was with that dreadful Titus woman."

This news displeased Charlotte, as she suspected it did Beryl, although it was impossible to be sure of her feelings these days.

She had been surprised a few days ago when her young friend showed her a letter from Mr. Yeates, who, after going many weeks without communicating, now informed her of his direction in town and proposed an immediate elopement. It was imperative, Beryl declared, that she speak with her importunate suitor, only how could it be achieved? When Charlotte realized that Beryl intended to break off her engagement, she had willingly offered to take her to town and had even undertaken the task of convincing Lord Rowan that he should permit his daughter a brief visit to London. She had kept him in the dark about Beryl's true purpose, winning his consent only when she hinted that the newly desirable union with Damon might result. But that was also her own wish, and it would likely be fulfilled if only she could bring the two together again.

After a maidservant took the Kinnards to their rooms, Mrs. Selby looked at her daughter and said accusingly, "That girl outshines you, Charlotte, you must realize that. And what of the brother? I suppose he has come to town only to get into trouble."

Charlotte said impatiently, "If Lady Beryl shines me down, what do I care? I am many years her senior and a spinster besides—I beg you to keep it in mind. I'm perfectly content to play the duenna. It's what I was doing down at Deerhurst while Damon was there."

Mrs. Selby returned to her needlework. After a brief silence she said with an injured air, "Your cousin is free of that Preston creature, and I've heard his Brighton flirtation with Georgiana Titus came to nothing. Mark my words, Charlotte, he'll be thinking of marriage soon."

"Oh, I do hope so," Charlotte said fervently. "But when he does, he won't be asking for my hand, that much I know."

Mrs. Selby dropped her embroidery hoop to press one hand to her thin bosom. "I should have guessed," she uttered in a voice of doom. "The sly creature! She came here to set snares for him, knowing she'll be right under his nose! Charlotte, how *could* you do this to me?"

The timely arrival of a footman spared Charlotte the necessity of a reply. Excusing herself, she left her mother moaning over her perfidy, and went to her room to compose a note for Beryl, asking Mr. Yeates to meet them in Hyde Park the following afternoon.

Long before the ladies emerged from their bed-chambers, Cedric took a hackney coach to the offices of Mr. Egerton, printer of novels and other literary works. Jane Austen had done him the favor of giving him a letter of recommendation to her own publisher, and *The Clandestine Betrothal*, now honed and polished to his satisfaction, was ready to be shown.

Much later in the day his sister and Charlotte also left the house in Brook Street, but they went in Mrs. Selby's elegant landaulet. It carried them to several shops and lastly to a silk warehouse where Beryl purchased material for the gown she would wear as Honoria's bridesmaid. From there they journeyed toward the park, arriving at the hour of the fashionable promenade; Charlotte, inured to the traffic and crowds which overwhelmed her companion, complained that London was a desert.

Beryl, eyeing the stream of vehicles passing through the Grosvenor Gate, wondered what she meant. When they entered London's pleasure-ground, she began scanning the throng for a gentleman with yellow hair. "How warm it is," she said. "Might we not alight and stroll in the shade of the trees?"

"What, and ruin our reputations?" cried Charlotte in mock reproof. "Walk about freely, when you can be driven in an endless and unvarying circle? La, child, you must be out of your senses!"

Beryl's laughter broke off suddenly, for she had noticed a clutch of young bucks nearby. "Why are those men staring?" she whispered.

"They deem it their bounden duty, yours being a new face, and a pretty one. Oh, Beryl, look at that love of a bonnet—the one Miss Sandys is wearing. Tomorrow let's go back to that milliner's in Jermyn Street, for I've decided I must have the hat we saw in the window. You remember the one—it was green taffeta lined with white silk, finished off with a single white plume."

"I thought it rather dear," said Beryl, unaccustomed to the prices of London goods. "I'd pay a fraction of the sum at Chichester."

"You wouldn't *find* such a bonnet at Chichester," the other lady said, nodding to a pair of females in a barouche. She continued her rapid commentary on the fashions on display, to which Beryl listened with only half an ear. "Now who can that man be?" Charlotte wondered aloud. "Twice we've passed him, and he bows and smiles as though he knows us. I've never seen him in my life, and I'm just as sure you have not."

When they passed him a third time, Beryl also noticed the fine beau. He wore a close-fitting coat of dark blue with gleaming buttons; pale pantaloons encased his legs like a second skin and disappeared into a pair of gleaming Hessian boots. The bright head was covered by a beaver hat, and he carried a malacca walking stick with a shiny gold knob. Something about him seemed familiar, but he was obviously a dandy, and as yet she was acquainted with none of that set. "I thought you knew everyone in London, Charlotte," she said, turning her head to catch another glimpse of the man over her shoulder. He bowed, placing his hand over his heart, and she clutched the side of the carriage.

"Whatever is the matter, Beryl? You look as though you've seen a ghost."

With a weak laugh, she answered, "I do believe I have."

"Please don't peer over your shoulder like that, or they'll accuse you of ogling the gentlemen,"

Charlotte said crisply. "Shall I direct John to pull up?"

"Yes, do. That man is Mr. Yeates."

Charlotte stared at her in abject astonishment. "It took you all this time to recognize him?"

Beryl said defensively, "Many months have passed since I last saw him, and besides, he never used to dress so fine." He was coming toward the landaulet, and without another word, she climbed down and went to meet him.

He took the hand she extended, clasping it tightly. "My lady—I was overjoyed to receive your note!"

Conscious of the passersby and Charlotte, observing them from the carriage, Beryl drew her hand away. The polished gentleman standing before her bore no resemblance to the unassuming suitor she had known in York, and she confessed, "I hardly knew you, you've changed so."

"For the better, I must hope. You had my letter? But of course, for here you are in London, just as I asked."

"Yes, but I—well, yes."

Lowering his voice to a conspiratorial whisper, Peter continued, "Will you walk with me? We've many plans to make."

She shook her head. "I mustn't leave Miss Selby. She is my friend, and we're staying at her mother's house in Brook Street."

"We?" he repeated, arching his brows.

"Two of my brothers came to town with me. Sid is lodging near Whitehall, but Ceddie—" She broke off, wondering what she'd said to make him frown.

Peter asked grimly, "Dear lady, can you slip away with so many people watching your movements?"

She gazed up at him worriedly, not quite knowing how to explain. "We cannot talk here. It is too difficult. Would it be convenient for you to call on me tomorrow?"

"I had hoped we might be on our way north by then—but you've given me an idea. Yes, I'll come to you in Brook Street, at any hour you name. I must go now," he said hastily, for a curricle drawn by a pair of matched bays was approaching.

"Two o'clock, then," Beryl told him, but she had the impression he hadn't heard her. Wondering what had attracted his attention, she turned her head and saw that a vehicle had drawn up beside the landaulet. The driver's icy blue eyes locked with Beryl's green ones, and the color ebbed from both faces.

Damon looked away from the young lady to greet his cousin, who smiled with pleasure as she extended her hand to him. "Mama told us you had lately returned from your travels. I ought to give you the cut direct, you deserve it for leaving Deerhurst so abruptly and then failing to write me a single line since then." She gave him no chance to reply, but went on airily, "I remained in Sussex until yesterday, and as you see, I've brought Lady Beryl home with me."

He said nothing, but transferred his murderous glance to Peter Yeates.

Charlotte viewed this as a promising sign of jealousy, which she hoped might spur him to action. "I wish we might talk longer," she said, "but you are blocking the carriageway and your popularity will suffer if you don't move on."

Damon urged his horses into a trot, and the staccato hoofbeats faded as the curricle vanished around a bend in the drive.

\* \* \*

After leaving his manuscript at Mr. Egerton's offices in Whitehall, Cedric partook freely of the many delights London offered a gentleman of his inquisitive nature. He visited an art exhibition and a museum bursting with antiquities, but his powers of observation were directed less toward the collections than the other people viewing them. Everywhere he went, he wrote his thoughts and impressions in the margins of his guide-book, and even when he sat in the Stranger's Gallery listening to a debate of the House of Commons, he scribbled notes to himself.

He assumed that his sister was as busy as he, enjoying a day of sophisticated jollification, and was therefore surprised by her silence throughout dinner.

"Lady Templetown's soirée is tomorrow," Mrs. Selby announced during the second course, "so I sent a footman to her house to inform her that Lady Beryl and Mr. Kinnard are with us."

"But I brought nothing suitable to wear at an evening party," said Beryl.

"Never mind," Charlotte told her. "My maid has clever fingers, she can shorten one of my dresses— I have a pretty blue silk which would become you well, far better than it ever did me."

The Selby household retired early that night, and before Cedric sought his own bed he crept along the hall to Beryl's door and tapped out an old code from their nursery days.

His sister, clad in her nightrail and a dressing gown, admitted him. "I thought you looked a bit sunk tonight," he explained. "What's the matter, did Mr. Yeates fail to meet you in the park?"

Reaching for her hairbrush, she said, "He was

there but we were interrupted, so he's calling on me tomorrow. I *am* feeling low," she confessed, "because seeing him again only confirmed that my affection for him was no more than an infatuation, and no basis for marriage. But I think he must still care for me, and I hate to hurt him by crying off."

"Do you want me there to support you?" Cedric offered.

She smiled at him gratefully but shook her head.

"Well, if Mr. Yeates does care for you, he's got a poor way of showing it. Didn't he sometimes go weeks and weeks without writing to you? And he never tried to see you, not once. Now he expects you to marry him in some hole-in-corner fashion, which is not only unfair to you but hardly likely to endear him to Papa."

Beryl could not deny any of this, reluctant though she was to blame Peter when she was so much at fault for tumbling into love with another man. But she couldn't think about Damon, or that painful episode in the park, so she asked Cedric how he had spent the day. After he had described his activities enthusiastically and in minute detail, she asked, "Why don't you escort Charlotte and me to the gardens at Kew tomorrow afternoon? I'm feeling so hemmed in by the city, a drive into the country will restore my spirits."

He said he would be happy to go with her, adding hopefully, "Unless, of course, Mr. Egerton should send for me."

Beryl spent the following morning so busily that she had little opportunity to dread her impending interview with Peter. First she tried on Charlotte's blue gown so the French maid could pin the hem and sleeves for alterations, and at midday Sidney arrived. He stayed no longer than a quarter of an hour, for he was on his way out of town and would board his transport to the Peninsula that evening.

The next caller, who entered the parlor to the accompaniment of the double chime from the long-case clock, was not only punctual but very cheerful. Casting about in her mind for a suitable opening, Beryl observed lamely, "It has been a long time since we met."

With his brightest, most winning smile, Peter Yeates replied, "Nearly four-and-twenty hours! It's been an eternity to me!"

She gazed at him blankly. "Since our encounter in the park, you mean? But I was speaking of the months that have passed since we parted in York."

When she indicated that he should sit, he chose the sofa cushion next to hers. "Now we are reunited," he said, "and soon, very soon, no power on earth will be able to separate us."

This was going to be more difficult than she had anticipated. "Mr. Yeates, I'm afraid you misunderstand my reason for coming to town. After reflection and careful consideration, I have come to the conclusion that we should not suit, and I therefore release you from the pledge we made so hastily."

Peter remained perfectly still, his brown eyes fixed upon the resolute little face before him. "You're crying off?" When she nodded, he asked, "Has your father ordered you to do so?"

"Papa knows nothing about it—yet," she answered. "I'm following the dictates of my own heart and conscience."

Narrowing his eyes, he asked harshly, "Are you quite sure you haven't been pressured into taking this step?" She shook her head in denial, but Peter didn't believe her. The fiendish Lord Elston must be responsible for her about-face, which had come at the worst possible time. Last month his grandfather had, without warning, stopped Peter's handsome allowance and now demanded that he return to York. He might even insist that his heir take a position of responsibility with the family firm, which dire fate Peter had narrowly avoided by battening on Lady Beryl last spring. Unless he married her, and quickly, he had no hope of placating his irate relative—and the many creditors pestering him for payment.

He must be careful not to reveal his alarm. It could be, he told himself, striving to keep calm, that her sentiments hadn't changed at all. If she doubted his devotion—and it occurred to him he had given her cause—she might be testing him. Young ladies deep in love were prone to such tricks, he'd heard.

"I blame myself for this," he declared sorrowfully. "I stayed away from Deerhurst only because I didn't want to anger your father. It wasn't easy to be patient, but I trusted in your constancy—and your fidelity—and I hope you trust in mine. Dear Beryl, why should we renounce one another now, when we can be wed by special license within a matter of days—hours!" He reached for her hand.

She pulled it away. "It cannot be, Mr. Yeates. I am sorry for it, but you must not persist."

When she climbed to her feet and put as much distance between them as the size of the room permitted, he cried, "Only give me the chance to redeem myself in your eyes. That is all I ask! You were not so cold in York."

"No, and I have come to regret it. We were too little acquainted to have made such a promise."

These words had the effect of a bucketful of cold water. After a brief silence, Peter said, "I am the heir of a very rich man; I can give you whatever you desire: jewels, carriages, a townhouse—anything."

Beryl's eyes flashed. "Do you think such an offer can sway me? Would you want to marry me if it did?"

"I want you as my wife on any terms. I have the license with me, we could—"

"Please say no more, Mr. Yeates."

"Do you think to have Lord Elston in my stead?" he demanded.

She whirled around to face him, her cheeks pink. "Lord Elston? He knows nothing of my affairs."

"Oh? Then why would he offer me five thousand pounds to jilt you?"

"Five thousand pounds?" she echoed. "I don't understand. What reason could he have for doing so?"

Seizing this welcome opportunity to discredit his enemy and rival, Peter hastened to enlighten her. "Some weeks ago your friend, the most noble marquis, invited me to his house in Berkeley Square. He offered me money, and in return I was supposed to give you up. Naturally I refused, for there was no mistaking his intentions toward you. Five thousand would be considered excessive for a female of wide experience, much less an untried girl." Peter, still not satisfied despite her dismayed expression, added, "His lordship told me in no uncertain terms that marriage was out of the question."

"It is too base—he would never—" But the fear that he might was enough to stifle Beryl's protest.

"I shouldn't ask," he went on, "and yet I cannot but feel I have a right to know. Just what is the nature of your attachment to Lord Elston, that he would take your compliance for granted?"

What a disagreeable man he was—very nearly as vile as Damon, whose behavior Beryl could not comprehend. "I have disclaimed our former bond," she told him tartly, "so I am not required to answer your allegation. We can have nothing more to say to one another, now or ever, so I ask that you leave this house."

She turned away, and after she heard him walk out of the room she crossed to the window and stood watching until she saw him round the corner of Brook and Davies Streets. When he was out of sight she wondered if she should cry now or later, or both.

Was she forever destined to be wrong in her judgements?

Peter, whom she had loved so dearly, however unwisely, was utterly despicable. Damon, once her friend and confidant, had amused himself by arousing her passions and then he abandoned her, and now he was breaking her heart a second time. He was no gallant and selfless Lord Llewellyn; his morals were far worse than he had acknowledged. If he truly believed she would consent to be his mistress, he was either excessively stupid, or so mad that he belonged under lock and key.

After drying her tears, she left the parlor to find Charlotte, knowing that her excuse for staying home from their expedition to Kew, a sudden sick headache, would be no fabrication.

*          *          *

Although she'd been able to beg off from the afternoon drive, Beryl could not avoid attending the soirée that evening. During the short drive to Lady Templetown's house in Portland Place, she listened absently to the battle of wills between Miss Selby and her mother.

"Now, Charlotte, do *try* to be conciliating tonight. This independent manner of yours isn't at all attractive to the gentlemen," Mrs. Selby said pettishly. "Mark my words, if you don't take care you'll suffer the fate of Lady Templetown's daughter. Past thirty now, and no hope of being wed."

"Sophia Upton detests society and is utterly indifferent to the male sex," Charlotte responded coolly. "She's a confirmed spinster and I will be greatly astonished if she even shows her face during tonight's entertainment."

The carriage drew up before Number Sixty-five, and Charlotte whispered to Beryl that the absence of a line of vehicles in Portland Place did not bode well for their chances of enjoyment. Beryl, her spirits too cast down for it to make a difference, smoothed her blue silk skirts and followed the other ladies to the front door.

Cedric and Beryl, knowing none of the other guests, kept to themselves. When Charlotte and her mother were accosted by friends, Beryl looked over at her brother and asked softy, "What news from Mr. Egerton?"

"I went to see him this afternoon," he admitted, "after Sid left us."

"And?"

"He says I've stuck Lady Frances with the wrong fellow after all."

"Oh, dear," Beryl said in quick sympathy. "But would he publish the novel if you altered it?"

"So he led me to believe, without promising anything outright. He says Thompkins is too young and idealistic to be a hero, he's not decisive enough and relies too much upon Lord Llewellyn. And, like Miss Jane, Mr. Egerton thinks the baron should win the lady because he's the one who saves her from scandal. Moreover, he says the female public will prefer a nobleman as the hero."

"I never thought of that."

"So I have made up my mind to let Llewellyn prevail," the young author declared. "Now that you've broken with Mr. Yeates, I suppose it makes no difference who Lady Frances marries."

With a shaky laugh, Beryl said, "Quite true! And frankly, I prefer that you change the book, now that I know Mr. Yeates is as full of false words as a dog is of fleas! Only don't lampoon him by making Thompkins too disagreeable, or he might sue for defamation of character!"

"Oh, I intend to publish under another name," said Cedric grandly.

She was conscious of the ironic aspect of the planned revision: Her fictional counterpart would now be united in marriage with the character based upon Damon. Lady Frances was thus assured the happy ending that Beryl could no longer dream of for herself, but she dared not admit this to the creator of Lord Llewellyn. And she worried that he was perceptive enough to realize that the marquis was responsible for her present woes, not Peter Yeates.

"Why, look," her brother said in a pleased voice, "Damon just came into the room—he's over there, talking to Charlotte."

Beryl had only a moment to recover her composure before she had to confront the very man she least wanted to meet; the prospect of conversing with him was abhorrent. In his dark evening clothes he looked like a devil with an angel's face, and his eyes glittered as bright as the diamond pin nestled in the snowy folds of his cravat. She could hardly meet them, knowing as she now did that after he had refused to marry her he'd offered her betrothed a sum of five thousand pounds, as though she were a piece of merchandise to be bartered for. He hadn't even been honest enough to come to her with his vulgar proposal, and she would never forgive him for the several ways he had shamed her. But she could have strangled her brother, who, after cataloguing the various sights he'd seen since coming to London, bolted for a refreshment table.

"Until I saw you in the park yesterday, I didn't know you'd come to town," Damon told her gravely. "Have you been here long?"

"Two days only." After a pause she added, "Sidney came with us, but he departed for Portsmouth today and is on his way back to the wars."

"I'm sorry I had no opportunity to say goodbye to him." When she made no reply, he filled the gap by asking, "Are you going to Whitehall to view the procession tomorrow? It promises to be a grand spectacle."

"Charlotte says I have no choice, it's my great chance to behold royalty," Beryl answered. "I didn't dare tell her I don't much care about princes and princesses, or seeing the spoils of war deposited in the chapel. My whole desire is to return to Deerhurst and help Honoria prepare for her wedding to Tracy."

"And what of your own wedding?" he asked,

and seemed to be holding his breath as he awaited her response.

Was he still so eager to have her for his mistress? Infuriated by his question and its implications, she lashed out at him, saying, "I've broken with Mr. Yeates, not that it's any of your business, my lord. And as it was *my* doing, not his, you may keep your five thousand pounds!"

She stayed only long enough to make sure her barb had found its mark. Seeing that his face had suddenly turned as starkly white as his neckcloth, she walked away, doubting that they would ever meet again, either in love or in anger.

Damon sent for his carriage immediately, and as it carried him back to Berkeley Square his thoughts were tumultuous.

He was relieved to know Beryl had broken her engagement and was no longer an unwitting pawn in Peter's game to win a fortune. He had a fair notion of the trials the young man would face upon his imminent return home; Damon had visited Peter's grandfather, the irascible merchant of York, during his recent stay in that ancient city. In common with most men of his class, the senior Yeates had looked askance upon his heir's activities—gaming, whoring, playing fast and loose with the fortune he'd labored hard to build—and had been even more disturbed by the report that the engagement to Lady Beryl Kinnard was hopeless. Damon, the sole witness to his wrath, knew the young wastrel would be reprimanded and punished for his many sins.

Upon his return to Elston House, he went directly to the library and filled a tumbler with brandy, hoping it would soothe his shattered nerves. It had been a shock, learning that Peter had used his offer of money against him as a weapon. It had been the parting shot of a desperate man. And as a result Beryl despised him; he'd read the truth in her face and voice, and most of all in her eyes.

Tonight she finished what he had begun the day he had left Deerhurst. Their association was over now, if it hadn't been already, and soon she would return to her loving father and her simple, happy life in Sussex. If only it were so easy for him, he thought, having realized long since that he would never cease to regret his inability to make her his wife. His life was a hell of his own devising, especially now that he burned with the desire rekindled by that painfully brief exchange in Lady Templetown's saloon. But the vengeful Peter had scuttled any chance of winning back Beryl's affections, had Damon possessed the courage to try.

After lengthy consideration, he reached for two sheets of writing paper, and as he took up his pen his ruling sense of self-preservation struggled with his need to see her once more and explain. She wouldn't receive him, though, so he scribbled several sentences, his quill sputtering and scratching across the blank page. He directed it to *London Gazette*, then wrote and addressed a second, equally curt announcement to the *Morning Post*.

When he was done, he didn't ring for a footman immediately, but reached for the decanter again, in no great hurry to send these messages on their way.

# 13

*Hope is banish'd*
*Joys are vanish'd,*
*Damon, my belov'd, is gone!*
—JOHN DRYDEN

Beryl, standing with her brother and Charlotte and the multitude of Londoners in either side of Whitehall, listened to a military band and waited for Queen Charlotte, the Duchess of York, and the royal princesses to show themselves at a window overlooking Horse Guards Parade. She feigned interest when the Prince Regent, mounted on a white charger, rode past, accompanied by his brothers the Duke of York and the Duke of Kent, and attended by several portly officers on horseback. And she tried to appear fascinated by the Trooping of the Colors.

But the unceasing play of the bands was tedious, and the formal presentation of the French eagles, five in number, seemed interminable. Two of them had been captured at Salamanca and two at Madrid; the other had been found at Ciudad Rodrigo, in the wake of General Massena's retreat. Four tattered standards and the blood-stained garrison flag from Badajoz were also paraded around the square to the lively strains of "The Grenadier's

March," while the Regent beamed as if he alone were responsible for taking these hard-won trophies. Several regiments of the Horse Guards led the procession into Whitehall Chapel, where the assembled dignitaries would hear divine service.

Beryl, eager to begin packing for her homeward journey, was glad when she and her companions returned to the house in Brook Street. Charlotte offered to assist her, overriding her feeble protests, and she had to maintain a flow of inane and light-hearted chatter as a barrier to any serious discussion, a feat as difficult as it was unsuccessful.

"Do you really mean to leave without telling me what Damon said to you last night?" Charlotte demanded.

"There's nothing to tell."

Unwilling to stand by and watch the desecration of a lawn chemise, Charlotte took the garment from Beryl's agitated hands and folded it herself, placing it atop the other items in the trunk. "I suspect my cousin is the cause of that haunted look you've been wearing all day. Are you so afraid to speak because you think I have a *tendre* for him? Truly, Beryl, Damon and I have never been more than good friends, and frequently much less. And don't waste your breath with denials—I was at Deerhurst all summer and was a witness to his courtship."

"It was naught but a—an agreeable flirtation," Beryl insisted. "He had no serious intentions."

"Flirtation!" Charlotte crowed. "My dear, if you think it was only that, you are far, far greener than I thought. You silly child, don't you know Damon is deep in love with you?"

But Beryl knew only that he had desired her, and she couldn't explain that to Charlotte, nor would she discuss the five thousand pounds and his plan to make her his mistress. "His attentions to me were a means of amusing himself while buried in the country," she said matter-of-factly, "and at the time I was far from certain of my own feelings. I thought I loved Peter and wanted to marry him, but then I began to know your cousin—and liked him better than I ought to have done." She followed this candid declaration with an off-center smile. "It seems I'm destined never to be sure of my own heart."

"You could be sure, if only you would stay. Why are you leaving so soon? I'd hoped to keep you a fortnight at least, not a mere three days!"

"You are town-bred, Charlotte, so I don't expect you to understand, but I miss Deerhurst desperately. And Papa even more."

Charlotte jerked her black head impatiently. "That's utter nonsense. You're running away from something—or *someone*—and homesickness is but a convenient excuse. Luckily for you, Deerhurst is as safe and remote as a nunnery. Oh, I don't doubt your distaste for London, or that you miss your family, and I agree it is much easier to go home than to meet Damon again, if you've quarrelled."

"I'm *not* running away!" Beryl cried, hurt by Charlotte's sarcasm. "Besides, Tracy and Honoria are to be married."

"But not until next month," Charlotte shot back. "You could stay longer, if you wanted to."

Beryl shook her head.

"Oh, I wish I could knock both your heads together to bring you to your senses!" said Charlotte in exasperation. She started toward the door, then turned around to say, "Mama says I should take care to control my unruly tongue, but I still believe that plain speaking does the most good. I mean no offense, Beryl, and I *do* know I could help, if only you'd let me."

When they met again at the tea table, both ladies were still suffering the effects of their earlier confrontation. With distant but meticulous politeness, they passed bread plate and butter, sugar and cream to each other and to Mrs. Selby. The older lady was oblivious to the tension on the other side of the table, letting her tea grow cold while she devoured the latest tidbits of gossip printed in a society journal.

She made both young ladies jump when she suddenly exclaimed in dreadful accents, "How *could* he! Oh, it's too, too unfair!"

Charlotte said irritably, "What could you possibly find in the Court Page to disturb you?"

Mrs. Selby presented a furious face to her daughter. "He is gone—*gone*, Charlotte, and without ever calling upon you. Oh, how dare he slight you—although it's entirely your own fault!" She held out the *Gazette*, pointing to the item that had incited her outburst. "Your cousin has retired to Elston Towers, and he's announcing it to all the town. Had you not wisdom enough to throw out even *one* lure at Lady Templetown's? He needs encouragement! How often must I tell you?"

Charlotte failed to dignify this with an answer and looked to Beryl. "Did you know? Did he mention his plans last night?"

Beryl shook her head, warning herself that it made no difference where Damon had gone. He would not trouble her again, and she ought to be glad of that. She finished eating her scone, avoiding Charlotte's piercing black eyes as they tried to read the secrets in her soul.

Mrs. Selby reached for the *Morning Post*. After a frantic search for its society column, she moaned. "Another notice! Why would he go into Wiltshire, of all places the most unlikely?" Looking over at Beryl, she said loftily, "Perhaps you may not be aware, my lady, but Elston is such a man of the town that when he sets foot as far as Hampstead, 'tis a wondrous thing! Wimbledon is the end of the earth to him."

Privately, Beryl thought the marquis showed to advantage in the country, but there was no point in saying so. Mrs. Selby embarked upon a lengthy and malicious tirade, and by the end of it Beryl had learned the names of all Damon's many lights of love: a prominent actress, a divorced baroness, the very married Lady Preston, and, most recently, the widowed Lady Titus.

The next morning there were two witnesses to the Kinnards' leavetaking, the street sweeper and a milkwoman bearing her yoke and pails; fashionable London had not yet begun to stir. After submitting to an embrace from the normally undemonstrative Charlotte, Beryl climbed into the hired post chaise and sank back against the cushions as it pulled away from the curb. Since learning of Damon's abrupt departure from town, Charlotte hadn't mentioned him again, and this tacit acceptance of what Beryl had known all along, that he was forever lost to her, was even more harrowing than yesterday's inquisition.

She envied Cedric his ability to sleep in a moving carriage, but suspected it was because he had been awake all night revising his novel. After he dozed off, she pondered everything that had happened to her during the brief visit to town, and concluded that she was fortunate to be free of all entanglements.

Lord Rowan's welcome was a hearty one, and his kiss upon her brow was a balm to her aching heart. During her absence from Deerhurst he'd been all alone, for Louisa was back at Fairdown with her brood, and Tracy was happily dancing attendance upon his future bride. Her father's eagerness to describe every occurrence, however minor, touched Beryl, and she smiled when he told her that another prize sow had borne her litter, the largest ever, and reported that the drains at the back of the house had been repaired with a minimum of difficulty and expense. There was an abundance of fruit this year, he declared—would she like to see? So Beryl accompanied him to the orchard, and was reluctant to spoil his pleasure in their reunion by telling him of her meeting with Mr. Yeates.

During dinner, Lord Rowan listened to his children's tales of London, and afterward he urged Beryl to play for him.

"Yes, of course, I will," she answered. "I brought some new music back with me and am eager to try it. But first I must explain to you why I went to town. Papa, while I was there I met with Mr. Yeates."

His lordship's craggy brows slanted downward in an angry frown. "I've told you I won't have you marrying him, and I meant it."

"I no longer think of marrying him," she said gently, "and told him as much, so you may be easy. I was wrong in my reading of his character and deeply regret making so hasty and ill-informed a choice. I've been justly punished for my folly, Papa." She did not add that after suffering disillusionment at the hands of two gentlemen, she would not be so quick to trust—or to love— again.

When she had revealed most of what had passed between her former suitor and herself, her father said gruffly, "I won't reproach you, but I wish you'd let me talk to him and spare you all that unpleasantness." He seemed to be distracted by something, and after she sat down at the pianoforte he asked whether she had met Lord Elston during her visit to town.

"Twice," she replied, lacing her fingers together. "He's in Wiltshire now."

"Is he? High time he took an interest in his estate," he said, nodding his head in a pleased fashion.

The following morning Beryl rode her mare to Fairdown to inform her sister of the termination of her engagement. Louisa, whose growing child inhibited her movements, wanted to hear all the details of her interview with Mr. Yeates, but Beryl omitted any reference to the marquis and his five thousand pounds.

Louisa's next question was an echo of her father's. "Tell me, did you see aught of Damon?"

Beryl had come home determined to forget him, only to have her family hamper that effort. "Did I fail to mention it?" she asked with an innocent air. "We met in the park one day, and also at Lady Templetown's soirée."

"That bore! You poor child, couldn't Mrs. Selby provide you with more interesting society than that of the Upton family? I can't imagine why Damon would attend a party of Lady Templetown's—he must have done so out of desperation. London can be very dull at this time of year."

As the days passed, activity helped to lessen Beryl's despondency, and with a wedding so near it was no time for long faces, although when she saw the engaged couple together it was impossible not to regret that she would never know the same happiness. Her favorite solitary pursuits—riding, walking, and gardening—were set aside as the festive day approached, and she was thankful to be diverted from speculation about how Damon was amusing himself in Wiltshire.

But she and her father had resumed their customary morning rides, and during one of them she was enough troubled by his grim, uncertain mood that she asked what was the matter.

"That Yeates fellow—you said he was angry about your jilting him. What if he took it into his head to come here and pester you?"

"I shouldn't think he would. Besides, you are here to protect me," she said, laughing off his fears for her safety.

"Yes, but I'm much occupied with estate business just now."

"My brothers are here."

The earl gave an impatient snort. "Much good they are! Ceddie is writing, writing, day and night, sometimes even forgetting his dinner, and Tracy has become quite a stranger, he spends so much of his time with Honoria. I think I must take steps for your protection, puss."

"What do you mean to do, chain me to the banister?" Beryl asked, amused. "Mr. Yeates is vulgar and impolite, but I don't believe he's dangerous, Papa."

"Any man is dangerous when he's thwarted. I

want you to be careful, and whenever you step beyond our gates, Smith or one of the other grooms must always go with you, d'you hear?"

Beryl knew better than to argue, but she doubted his alarms would outlast the week.

A few days later, while tramping through the Home Wood with Gypsy tagging at her heels, she was accosted by Bob Rowley, who popped out from behind a large tree, cap in hand. He startled the spaniel far more than he did Beryl.

"Might I have a word with your ladyship?" he asked.

"Yes, of course. Oh, *do* be silent!" she rebuked the dog, now barking frantically at Beryl's former playmate.

"I wanted to tell you there's a stranger lurking hereabouts," Bob said, bending down to scratch Gypsy behind her ears. "Mind, I've not seen 'im myself, but I heard as how he stopped at Singleton yesterday, and the barkeep at the Fox and 'ounds suspicioned he was bound for Deerhurst."

"What manner of man was he?"

"My friend says he was a yellow-haired cove, a gentleman in speech and dress, and seemed mighty interested in the goings-on with Master Tracy's wedding to Miss Honoria. The earl bade me keep my winkers open, he's that worried about some-one abductin' your ladyship, and so I shall." Bob, taking note of Beryl's worried expression, added in less dire accents, "To be sure, there's naught to fear, nor will there be, even if this fellow should be up to no good. But I thought it might be best to let you know, my lady, so you might keep on your guard 'gainst ruffians and such-like."

"You were quite right to warn me," she said, wondering how she was expected to deal with a ruffian if she met one. "How long did the gentleman stop at Singleton?"

"Long enough for a mug o' ale."

"Well, if you should hear any more of this person, I hope you will inform me." She nodded farewell to Bob and continued down the path with the frisking spaniel. This yellow-haired stranger who had been seen creeping about the district could be Peter Yeates, and if he had been ruthless enough to suggest an elopement, it was entirely possible that he might contemplate an abduction.

She was sufficiently concerned to take a precautionary measure of her own, and when she returned to the house, she went directly to the estate office and took the key to the gun room.

When the time had come to teach his children how to handle firearms, the earl had made no distinction between Cedric and Beryl, who had shared her brother's lessons in marksmanship. On one of her birthdays her father had presented her with a small, silver-mounted pistol engraved with her initials, which reposed in a pretty tortoise-shell box. Nowadays it went unused for years at a time, but Beryl knew her delicate but deadly weapon could ensure her protection as well as a dozen stalwart grooms, if not better.

After a long journey from his parish in Northumberland, the Reverend Richard Kinnard arrived at Deerhurst to preside over his brother Tracy's nuptials. The cleric's merry laugh and humorous gray eyes seemed to belie his sober calling, but he also possessed an innate kindness and a true devotion to the church. Several years senior to Beryl and Cedric, he had proved his academic brilliance at Oxford, where he had taken two degrees, and owed his comfortable living to a maternal uncle, a duke with vast holdings in the north. The present dissension and unrest among the laboring classes had plagued many northern towns, and that night he described the riots and machine-breakings to his family.

When they retired to the drawing room after dinner, he abandoned this troubling subject to ask, "What kept Louisa and Roger away? Did no one invite them to dine? A paltry homecoming, this, with only the squirrel and Ceddie and the bridegroom to receive me!"

"I sent Smith over to Fairdown with a message," his father replied, "but Louisa gave him some excuse. She might be in a delicate situation, but she ought to be able to travel a bare five miles to see her brother, and so I shall tell her."

Tracy, smiling enigmatically, stroked his handsome side whiskers, a relic of his military career. "I daresay she is recruiting her energies."

Beryl, who scented a mystery, cried, "If you're keeping some secret, I'll manage to uncover it, by fair means or foul!"

"You'd best not try, it might spoil an agreeable surprise," he answered calmly.

By the time she went to bed, she had forgotten Tracy's curious remark. As usual at the end of a long day, she was inclined to reflect upon her own affairs. The return of the lighthearted Richard had lifted her spirits, and their father no longer seemed preoccupied by fears that she might be snatched up unawares by Peter Yeates and carried off.

If not completely happy, she was at least as content as any female in her position could expect to be. The man she loved was denied to her, but so be it; she had too much spirit to give way to mel-

ancholy and throw herself into the marble fountain like a modern-day Ophelia.

But Deerhurst would not always be her home,
she thought, because one day her eldest brother
Tom would inherit, and his high-nosed wife would
take over the management of the household. Beryl
doubted her ability to recede into the woodwork;
the possibility of becoming a nonentity in her beloved home was disturbing. Since she was not
going to be married, she must begin to form some
sort of plan for her future. And as she lay in her
bed, it occurred to her that Cedric would eventually require an establishment of his own. They
could find a country cottage not unlike the one at
Chawton where the Austen ladies lived so cozily,
and she could keep house for her brother while he
wrote his novels.

She wondered whether the single ladies of her
acquaintance—Charlotte and the two Miss Aus-
tens and the doctor's homely sister—had ever suffered a disappointment in love. Somehow they
had learned to value their independence above
any other tie save that of blood. Did such resigna-
tion come with age? After one heartbreak, or
several?

That night in her dreams she was visited by the
one responsible for breaking her own heart, as she
often was. But he did not come to her as the cold,
cruel persona of her nightmares, but as the tender
and loving Damon who had once wooed her with
sweet words and soft caresses, and he said everything she had longed to hear that day in the cottage on the marsh.

It was a delightful but disturbing fantasy, and
as Beryl felt herself being inexorably pulled toward

consciousness, she closed her eyes tightly, trying to ease herself back into sleep. His arms had seemed so strong and real, and her longing was so intense, that tears sprang to her eyes.

# 14

*Come, let us now resolve at last*
*To live and love in Quiet.*
                    —JOHN DRYDEN

On the day before the wedding a terrible foreboding gnawed at Beryl. That night there would be a dinner in honor of the forthcoming marriage, and she would serve as her father's hostess, a prospect so daunting that she expected to derive little pleasure from the party. The lavish entertainments of the summer had set a standard she feared she could never meet, and although she half hoped Louisa might drive over from Fairdown to offer advice and assistance, her only caller was the bride herself.

Honoria, her lovely face strained, confessed that she had made an escape. "I slipped out of the house as soon as Mama began arguing with my aunt about what sort of flowers should decorate the church. So I harnessed the horse and gig myself, like the good farmer's wife Tracy expects me to be, and left before anyone could stop me."

"If you came here seeking my brother, you came in vain," Beryl replied, "because Dick and Ceddie bore him off this morning on some spree." When Honoria frowned, she said soothingly, "Nothing of a shocking nature—Dick is a parson, after all! And I'm sorry you missed Tracy, but you'll see him tonight, and every day of your life after tomorrow." She forgot her own nervous fears and fancies as she tried to calm the skittish bride. "I had a new gown made at Chichester and it's just arrived—I haven't even opened the box yet. Come up and have a look," she invited her.

Honoria admired the evening frock of rosebud pink but pointed out sorrowfully that the seamstress had neglected to trim the sleeves and neck.

"Charlotte Selby would say it's what I should have expected of a provincial dressmaker," Beryl sighed. "But it doesn't matter. No one will notice me tonight; all eyes will be on the bride!"

"That isn't true," Honoria contradicted her, "for you will preside over the party." With a graceful flick of her hand, she ordered Beryl to turn around. "Slowly, slowly. Oh, dear, and it looks even worse from the back. That style of sleeve is too plain without a bit of lace."

"I suppose I might take it back to Chichester for alteration," Beryl said reluctantly. Then her face brightened with another idea. "If only I had some trim, one of the maids might sew it on after ironing the table linens." She thought for a moment. "Louisa's got a length of old Brussels. I can ride over to Fairdown and ask if any is left." Removing the pink silk gown, she exchanged it for her morning dress of sprigged muslin.

"But Fairdown is all of five miles away, nearly as far as Chichester," her friend protested. "Let me drive you to Rowan village instead. Miss Shenstone is bound to have some lace, even if it's only Nottingham or Honiton. You don't need much."

Beryl, crossing to the dresser to retrieve her

bulging reticule, said shrewdly, "There's something at Fairdown that you and Tracy are desperate to keep hidden from me. What is it?"

"Nothing. That is to say, I can't imagine what you're talking about," Honoria said evasively. "Shall we go now?"

It was only a short drive to Dr. Shenstone's brick-faced house; it sat across the road from the church in which Miss Capshaw would become Mrs. Kinnard on the morrow. After a long search through her sewing box, the doctor's sister produced some lace, and when she learned how it would be used she would accept no reimbursement and begged her ladyship to let it be a gift in honor of the wedding. She was a talkative soul, so the errand took rather longer than either young lady had expected.

Beryl parted from Honoria at the front gate, saying, "You needn't take me home. I'm sure I would benefit from a long walk. Apart from running up and down the stairs to the kitchen and the scullery, I had no exercise this morning." After waving goodbye, she set out along the path which wound through the woods.

Beryl hoped the fine weather would hold for the wedding. It was a brilliantly sunny day; the leaves nearest the tops of the trees had begun to turn, and a few were already drifting to the ground. As she passed the Rowley cottage, she wondered if Bob had heard anything more about the stranger he'd mentioned the other day, and when her sharp ears caught the sound of cracking twigs in the distance, she merely supposed her father's pigs had been driven into the wood to forage for acorns. Nor did she feel particularly alarmed when she first heard footsteps; she was accustomed to meeting Bob Rowley, who always chose this way home in preference to the main road.

But what if it wasn't Bob? Beryl paused just long enough to remove the tiny silver-mounted pistol from her reticule. Its cold weight in her hand was reassuring, and she walked on toward a fork in the path.

A man stood there, and the sun at his back threw his face into shadow. The cut of his clothes proved he wasn't Bob, so she raised her weapon and pointed it at him, saying firmly, "Come no closer, sir, or I shall put a bullet through you."

"I realize I am trespassing, *petite*, but would you really shoot an unarmed man?" he inquired in a gentle but carrying voice.

She was so startled that she dropped her pistol. The gentleman approached, stopping only when he was near enough for her to see that his eyes were the color of woodland bluebells. "Why are you here?" She hurled the question at him, affronted by his unexpected presence.

"I was invited to the wedding. Did you think your brother's oldest friend would be excluded from tomorrow's festivities?"

As it dawned upon her that Damon had come from the direction of the Meriden estate, she asked, "Are you the great mystery of Fairdown?"

"I don't know about that, but I am staying with Roger and Louisa. Did no one tell you?"

She shook her head. "How foolish of Tracy and Honoria to hide the truth from me. Their wedding day might have been that of your funeral, my lord." Not that she would have pulled the trigger, even if he had been Peter Yeates.

"Why do you carry a pistol?" Damon asked, bending down to retrieve it.

"Papa insists that I take precautions when I go out. And when Bob Rowley told me a fair-haired gentleman was seen at the Fox and Hounds, I thought it might be Peter come to frighten me."

A sudden peal of laughter shattered the deep silence all around them. "Oh, my sweet life, *I* am that fair-haired traveler. What a blow to my vanity to learn that the suspicion never crossed your mind!" When his mirth subsided, he asked, "Are you frightened of Yeates? You've no cause to be, for he's back in Yorkshire by now, receiving the scold of his life for failing to secure a nobleman's daughter as his bride." When she gazed back at him incredulously, he explained, "Peter's grandfather promised to settle a fortune on him if he married into the peerage."

"How do you know that?"

"Both of them admitted it to me, each in his own fashion. I had the felicity of meeting the elder Yeates when I was in York for the August Meeting." Damon could see that she was considerably taken aback by this information, and therefore chose not to reveal the full extent of Peter's duplicity—the gambling, the many infidelities.

"I don't want to talk about Peter, or—or anything else," she said stiffly. "I must be on my way, or Papa will wonder what has become of me."

He blocked her way, and when she tried to step around him he grasped her wrist. "Please wait. I must speak with you," he said.

"I'll see you this evening. Aren't you coming to our dinner for Tracy and Honoria?"

"Yes, but we may not have an opportunity to speak privately. I walked all this way just to see you. It must be a full three miles across country."

"Then I suggest you ride next time; it's much quicker," she shot back.

"Beryl, I—"

"No," she said flatly. "I won't listen. As a guest in my home and at the wedding you are entitled to common civility from me. But we aren't in company at present, and I can do as I please. I don't wish to be alone with you now or in future, and I hope you will remember it. Good day, my lord."

He released her, and she walked past him without another word.

She was as lovely as ever, and Damon was piqued by the discovery that she hadn't fallen into a decline over his neglect. The distant, unemotional creature making her way through the wood bore no resemblance to the merry, laughing girl who had once kissed him so ardently. Did she no longer care for him? he wondered, watching her go. Had he lost—or relinquished—his power to make her smile?

The mild October sun warmed Beryl's back as she knelt upon the ground, her muslin gown protected by a faded brown smock. A trug filled with lavender stalks sat upon the grass, her discarded secateurs beside it, and now she was spreading mulch around her thriving plants. Her labors were familiar enough that she could perform them unthinkingly, which was fortunate, because her mind ran unceasingly upon her brief reunion with Damon.

His presence was far from welcome, but she could maintain her composure so long as she met him in a social setting, surrounded by family and friends. But the strong surge of emotion she'd experienced when he had materialized in her path told her that she still cared, far too much for her own good. He was a tantalizing combination of strength and gentleness; he possessed wit and charm. But his crude attempt to bargain with Peter Yeates had revealed two unfortunate but inescapable truths: His only interest in her was carnal; and he would never allow himself to form a lasting attachment to any woman.

Her task completed, Beryl gathered up her tools and moved on to the next grouping of plants. The thick leather gloves inhibited her efforts to pluck the smaller weeds, so she tossed them aside. As she plunged her bare fingers into the cool, damp soil, she became aware of another presence and looked up to find Damon watching her from a bench flanked by two urns. Perhaps, she thought wearily, as she went on with her work, she should listen to whatever he was so determined to say. Then he would leave her alone.

"Now that I've run you to ground again, my little fox, I hope you'll hear me out, because I have something important to ask you."

She turned her frowning face upon him. "I have an idea what it might be, and the answer is no. I rate myself much higher than five thousand pounds. You can buy many things with your fortune, my lord, but never me."

In three brisk strides Damon covered the distance between them. "What exactly did that devil Yeates tell you?" he demanded.

"That you offered him purchase money, that you tried to—to buy me. He believes that you—that I—that we—" She ripped a clump of grass from the earth, creating a small shower of dirt. "He insulted me," she concluded, her cheeks flaming. "He asked if I'd been your mistress during your visit to Deerhurst."

"I'm not surprised. He said much the same to me."

"You're the one I despise the more," she continued in a shaking voice. "Bartering for me as though I were a—a common whore!"

"Yeates lied." She eyed him in patent disbelief, and he added, "Oh, I did offer him the money, that much was true, but not for the reason he said. I tried to bribe him into releasing you from that engagement, and I would have paid any sum, done anything to keep you away from him after I learned what he was: a liar, a gamester, an utter reprobate." Taking her roughly by the arm, he forced her to stand up and face him, and though she struggled, he would not let her go. "My precious idiot, why would you believe I wanted to purchase your favors? *I'm* insulted that you should even suspect me of such baseness!"

Beryl's heart was perilously close to bursting with relief. "Well, after all your talk about the Lovell curse, and never wanting to marry, what else could I think?"

"I *am* cursed, God knows, and have been ever since I made those rash statements." Releasing her arm, he dropped down upon his knees. "Behold me at your feet, desperate for your pardon. I was as wrong that day as I ever was in my life, Beryl, and every hour since then I have regretted my stupidity."

Slightly mollified by his extravagant show of remorse, she said softly, "I forgive you. Do get up— the gardeners might see you."

"Forgiveness isn't sufficient," he said, rising. "Marry me, Beryl."

For a moment she thought it was her imagination at work, but looking up at his face, so pale and tense, she knew she hadn't misheard him. "Your apology is welcome, and that I have accepted, but the proposal isn't at all necessary."

"Yes, it is. Hear me out—though I don't quite know where to begin, for lovers, like dying men, may well at first disordered be."

"Oh, Damon," she said impatiently, "if you're going to quote poetry at me and pretend to be mad in love, it won't move me. I had my fill of that sort of thing from Peter."

"You accuse me of dissembling?"

"Yes, and of offering marriage because you feel you must make some kind of reparation. But you needn't, because I've formed another plan for my future. When Ceddie becomes famous, as he will surely do, I mean to keep house for him. He can write great books, and I'll raise flowers and pigs, and—oh, don't look at me like that!" she cried in despair. "I crave peace and quiet. I've been thinking of your cousin Charlotte, of Miss Austen and her sister Jane at Chawton—they are all perfectly happy. Miss Shenstone, too."

"Who?" he asked, as if bemused by this barrage of names.

"The doctor's sister. You met her last summer."

"A dish-faced female with a tongue that runs on wheels? I don't perfectly understand what you have in common with her."

She would have explained it, but she had just realized that if she were so independent of him, she wouldn't have to work so hard to convince them both. When his arms closed around her she gave a small cry, pushing and pounding him with her dirt-stained fists, but clearly he didn't believe in her distress. His lips moved across her face, taking her mouth hungrily, forcing her to respond.

He lifted his head, and his smile was triumphant and slightly mocking. "I ask you, was that the act of a man bent on contracting a marriage of convenience?"

"Oh, Damon," she murmured, shaking her head at him in disappointment. "You equate passion with love. You've decided that your only hope of getting me into your bed is to take me with the full sanction of church and society. And though I should be flattered, I'm not. And I won't marry you."

"You proposed to me first, Beryl," he reminded her, "and while you were honor-bound to another man. I won't believe you are indifferent."

She could not meet his eyes, but neither could she lie to him. "I've never claimed to be."

"Then why do you refuse?"

"Because I'm no more cut out for marriage than you are. When I first knew Peter I thought I loved him, and if I could mistake my heart once, I might do it again, many times. Nor do I want to repeat my sufferings of last summer, when you made me love you and then deserted me."

He captured her fluttering hand. "Beryl, I was so unsure of myself then, I didn't dare make promises I didn't know if I could keep. Please don't turn my own words against me. That is the worst punishment you could possibly inflict, and it's beyond bearing. I don't just want you. I love you. And you won't regret marrying me; I'll make sure of it. You'll see, I'm going to be a model husband." As if to prove it to her, he took out his handkerchief and began rubbing the dirt from her fingers.

Recalling one impediment to a happy future at his side, Beryl said sadly, "I could never live in town."

"I'll not ask it of you." Smiling down at her he added, "But one day I hope to convince you that London is more than dull parties in Portland Place, and promenading in the Park, and gossip. I'm sure there are many things you would enjoy as I do—the opera, the theaters. The concerts."

Once again she found herself at *point-non-plus*, though only temporarily. "You would expect me to look the other way and pretend ignorance of your flirts and—and your other friends," she said meaningfully, her color high.

"You are my only flirt," he said, clasping her hand tightly and placing it over his heart. "My only friend. Before you became the sole object of my desire, I consorted with women I couldn't possibly marry as a form of protection, I was that devoted to my carefree life, but no more. After I left Deerhurst, I traveled the country, going from Brighton to London to York and back, and lastly to Elston Towers. And you know why I went there? Not to escape you, however often I told myself it was the reason. I had to make sure that the place was worthy of you, and I mooned about my estate like a lovesick schoolboy, picturing you there. My house *is* beautiful, I'm even rather proud of it, yet to me it seemed more hollow and empty than I remembered. It cries out for you, just as I do." Tenderly he smoothed a curl from her brow. "Optimistic fellow that I am, I have lately purchased the finest pianoforte to be had in all England, and it waits for you in Wiltshire."

Oh, why must he have an answer for her every argument, and the very ones which made her doubt the wisdom of her persistent refusals? She would be well served indeed if he took her at her word. And she was on the point of giving him the answer he sought when she recalled a bar to marriage that neither of them could overcome. "Papa is so stubborn," she sighed. "He likes you very well, and he would regard any suitor as an improvement over my last one, but he won't permit me to leave him."

"He didn't seem to be so terribly alarmed by the prospect."

"You haven't spoken with him?" she gasped.

He nodded. "We concluded our discussion a short time ago. Don't look so shocked, I had to ask your father's permission first—even Yeates did that. The notions you cherish about my character appall me, Beryl."

"Papa gave his consent?"

"Naturally. I'm a very good catch, although you seem to think otherwise. I would even go so far as to describe him as pleased, and he asked me why I took so long to apprise him of our plans."

"*Our* plans?"

Damon ignored this outburst. "You know, I think you're right; your last *affaire* must have reconciled him to the inevitability of your marriage. I can almost be grateful to that blackguard lover of yours for smoothing my path, although not to the extent that I regret knocking him down."

"You struck Peter? I wanted to," Beryl confessed. "But what else did Papa say? I can't believe he would give me up, just like that."

"Oh, he's not giving you up, he's only sharing you with me. He suggested that we announce the betrothal tonight, but I couldn't agree to it until I had seen you." Seeing that her brow was creased by thought, he asked, "What is your answer?"

"But the party is for Tracy and Honoria."

"I meant an answer about marrying me," he laughed, holding her against his heart.

"Damon, the gardeners will see us."

"So you keep saying, but I don't give a damn about the gardeners," he growled.

Beryl giggled. "That is quite obvious. Stop, Damon, we mustn't—not here. Would you want a large wedding or a small one?"

He stopped nuzzling her neck to say, "I don't like weddings, although the notion of a honeymoon appeals to me very strongly. I want to be married immediately, and with absolutely no fuss. Justin was kind enough to procure a special license from the Bishop of Bath and Wells, and I brought it with me. All your family are here, and Tracy and Honoria won't be leaving for Kent till the end of the week. Let's follow them to the altar a few days from now—Richard can tie the knot."

"Oh, I don't know," she murmured.

He heaved a sigh of loving exasperation. "Have I bared my soul to no avail? What objection are you about to dredge up now?"

She smiled back at him, her eyes bright. "There is one thing I must know before I can accept your proposal, my lord. You told me once that you thought of employing that horrid Humphrey Repton to improve the landscaping at the Towers. Is that still your intention?"

Taking her face between his hands, Damon answered, "Oh, no, not any longer. For it is you, Beryl, who will make my garden."

# 15

*Where love is planted there it grows*
*It buds and blossoms most like a rose*
*It has a sweet and pleasant smell*
*No flower on earth can it excel.*
—SUSSEX FOLK SONG

The narrow, towering chimneys which gave Damon's country house its name were visible for many miles away, and he eyed them wistfully throughout a long morning spent with his dour bailiff, overseeing the annual sheep dipping. Despite being thirty-two years old and master of all he surveyed, man and beast, he felt like a lad floundering at his lessons as he asked yet another question which made his companion shake his grizzled head dolefully. Taking pity on the old fellow, who was so patiently trying to instill in him the rudiments of sheep-farming, he excused himself, saying he would return on the morrow, and pointed his horse's head toward home. Each changing season brought a whole new set of tasks, and his studies in estate management were often tedious in the extreme. Still, he persevered, not only because he wished to earn the respect of his people, but also because he aspired to a success comparable to Beryl's. For she reveled in her duties as mistress of his grand, sprawling house, performing them with grace and aplomb, as though she had been bred to become chatelaine of so large an establishment.

When he reached the stables he dismounted with unseemly haste. Oblivious to the grin splitting the face of the groom who took charge of his thoroughbred, he made his way across the lawn to a summer house overlooking the gardens. His wife invariably spent her mornings there, reading or sewing or penning letters to her extensive family.

He found her seated before a writing table, her brown head bowed. She was wearing a gown of sea-green muslin to complement the necklace of glass beads he'd bought for her at the Rowan village fair just over a year ago. "You look like a water nymph, *petite*."

Looking up, she laughed at him. "And yesterday I was a rosebud. Will you never cease to offer me commonplace flattery, Damon?"

He kissed the enticing portion of bare neck exposed by the latest mode in hairdressing, glancing over her shoulder at the letters spread out before her. "Has everyone we know united to bury us in correspondence?"

She picked up a handful of notes and made a fan of them, peeping over it playfully. "Choose one, my lord, and I'll reveal its message." When Damon pointed to the note bearing his father-in-law's scrawled frank, she sighed and shook her head. "Papa complains of your absence from the House of Lords, and urges you to take your seat at least once before the session ends."

"Sorry though I am to disappoint him, there are

other things I'd rather do. Mostly with you," he added provocatively, just to make her blush.

Within hours of being declared husband and wife by her reverend brother, Damon had brought his bride to Wiltshire, where they had remained in blissful seclusion for the past nine months. After graciously welcoming them to the ranks of the married, the Cavenders and the Blythes had tried to interest them in neighborhood activities; Damon had become a subscribing member of the local hunt, and Beryl joined Nerissa and Miranda as a patroness of the charity school. But they seldom strayed beyond their lodge gates for anything more than an informal dinner party at Cavender Chase or at the Blythe manor house. During a long, cold winter they had kept one another warm, and even on the most inclement days they had ventured into the garden, Beryl's face peeping delightfully from her furs. She had been a rabbit then, all soft brown curls and quivering nose, enchanting Damon anew in that ice-bound season. Previously a stranger to the pleasures of true companionship, he never ceased to wonder at his former preference for solitude. They passed the chilly evenings reading aloud to each other, or talking until the candles guttered; together they made sweet music with the violin and pianoforte, and sweeter music still in the great tented bed. In the spring they had rejoiced over the birth of a son and heir at Cavender Chase, standing as godparents to the squalling and affronted infant. Now it was summer, when every hour not spent outdoors was unendurable.

Reaching out to touch another of Beryl's letters, he asked, "And what does Louisa say in her weekly report from Sussex?"

"Lolly is as sweet as ever. She has enslaved her father and brothers, and Papa positively dotes on her. I have been eclipsed in his affections by my own niece!" Beryl handed him several sheets, saying, "This comes from Charlotte. She says Ceddie is lionized wherever he goes in London. Just think, everyone is talking of his Lord Llewellyn and Miss Jane's Mr. Darcy! I doubt that our Chawton friend will remain unknown for much longer, her *Pride and Pejudice* is so popular. She wrote, too, to say she would be in London this autumn." Eyeing her husband uncertainly, she said, "We agreed, did we not, to go up to town when the Cavenders do? I thought we might invite them to stay with us at Elston House, if you don't object. There is plenty of room, isn't there, for Juliet and little John?"

"Indeed there is. Justin and I were talking last night, and he says Granville Leveson-Gower is urging him to bestir himself again now that Canning has relinquished the party leadership. There's bound to be another reshuffling of ministers, and Justin has always dreamed of a government post."

"You're always saying Mira would make the perfect political hostess, and I must admit, she seems very hopeful about Justin's prospects."

"What about you, *petite*? Are you quite sure you want to visit loathsome London?" he teased.

"Oh, yes," she said eagerly.

"I could very well change my mind, if there's the smallest chance that Ceddie might reveal that I was the inspiration for that plaster saint of a hero, Llewellyn. If ever you doubt the depth of my devotion, my love, just remember that I stood by you even *after* I learned my courtship had been painstakingly documented by your whelp of a brother."

"Just think of poor me, the model for that foolish Lady Frances! I like Miss Jane's rational Lizzie Bennet far better, even though she was taken in by that nasty Mr. Wickham." When Damon failed to smile, she asked, "Do you dislike Ceddie's novel so much?"

"No, not that. I just recalled a bit of news Justin told Dominic and me on our way back from that county dinner last night. I meant to tell you when I got home, but I forgot. You *made* me forget," he added, his voice heavy with accusation.

She dimpled back at him. "You were just as eager as I. What is your news?"

"A friend of yours was married last week."

"Another wedding! First Tracy and Honoria— oh, Damon, she is increasing, I'm so jealous—and now Charlotte and Sidney admit to having been engaged since last summer! She's so proud of his promotion to major after the battle of Vittoria, and—" Realizing she had digressed from the subject, Beryl said, "I can't imagine who could have been married recently, for everyone I know is already matched."

"It was Peter Yeates."

Her mouth fell open in astonishment. "But that's unfair—he's not exactly a *friend*. Who is his bride?"

"Also an acquaintance of ours: Lady Martha Onslow."

"But how did they ever meet one another?"

"Lady Martha was staying at Harrogate with the Wainworths, who went there to take the waters last month," Damon explained. "They eloped to Gretna Green."

"So Peter *has* wed an earl's daughter, just as his grandfather wanted," she mused. "It has been so long since I've thought about him. Well, I can't imagine he would make a very comfortable husband."

Damon walked over to the open window, and placing his hand on the sill, he asked, "Do you ever think about last summer?"

"Sometimes," she said, puzzled by his gravity.

"I shall never forget our picnic at Selsey, the darkest day of my life. Today I was reminded of it, as I always am when I come upon an obstacle which seems insurmountable. I'm new to the role of great landowner. I envy Justin and Dominic their talent for dealing with tenants and laborers. I stayed away from the Towers far too long and must pay the price. I realize that. And yet I know my present worries are as nothing compared to what I felt at the prospect of living my life without you."

Beryl went to stand beside him and covered his hand with her own. Softly she said, "It is the same with me, Damon." Together they gazed out at the flowers dancing in the breeze. "And I will always regret my silly objections to marriage the day you proposed. As much as I loved you, I didn't guess that we would be every bit as happy as Lord Llewellyn and Lady Frances in Ceddie's book. And we are, aren't we?"

Her sweet face was turned up to him like a blossom seeking the sun. "Much happier," he corrected, before touching his lips to hers.